CUM FOR ME 8
Lickety Split

Sugar E. Walls

Lock Down Publications & Ca$h Whispers
Cum for Me 8

Lock Down Publications
Po Box 944
Stockbridge, Ga 30281

Visit our website at **www.lockdownpublications.com**

Copyright 2021 by Sugar E. Wallz
Cum for Me 8

First Edition December 2021
Printed in the United States of America
This is a work of fiction. Names, characters, places, and incidents either are products of the author's imagination or are used fictitiously. Any similarity to actual events or locales or persons, living or dead, is entirely coincidental.
Book interior design by: Shawn Walker
Edited by: Tamira Butler

Stay Connected with Us!

Text **LOCKDOWN** to 22828 to stay up-to-date with new releases, sneak peaks, contests and more…

Thank you!

Submission Guideline.

Submit the first three chapters of your completed manuscript to ldpsubmissions@gmail.com, subject line: Your book's title. The manuscript must be in a .doc file and sent as an attachment. Document should be in Times New Roman, double spaced and in size 12 font. Also, provide your synopsis and full contact information. If sending multiple submissions, they must each be in a separate email.

Have a story but no way to send it electronically? You can still submit to LDP/Ca$h Presents. Send in the first three chapters, written or typed, of your completed manuscript to:

LDP: Submissions Dept
Po Box 944
Stockbridge, Ga 30281

DO NOT send original manuscript. Must be a duplicate.

Provide your synopsis and a cover letter containing your full contact information.

Thanks for considering LDP and Ca$h Presents.

Sugar E. Walls

Chapter One

Thug Luvin

Just the mere thought of him walking through the door had my pussy wet and my clit pulsing. My nipples painfully strained against the T-shirt I had on, his T-shirt. I could smell his aroma, as if it had been etched into the fabric itself. The thought of his dark-chocolate skin against my milky flesh had me on edge. I wasn't sure how much longer I could have waited for him, so I decided to entertain myself until he got there.

I spread my legs and slid my panties to the side. My clit peeked out from between my pussy lips, letting me know it wanted to be touched. I pulled the hood back and exposed the raw flesh underneath. Before I touched it, I slid my middle finger into my wet hole and coated it with my juices. When I pulled it out, I put it on my clit and pressed as hard as I could.

"Mmm, yes." A low moan escaped from deep within as I massaged it in slow, circular motions, thrusting my hips to the rhythm.

I didn't even hear him come in, but I felt his finger slide inside of me. "This what you been waiting for?" he whispered.

I didn't open my eyes because I didn't need to. I was familiar with his touch because I had never felt another like it.

"Yes baby," I responded and continued. "I was just getting this pussy ready for you." I smiled as he glided his finger in and out of me as my pussy gripped him tightly.

I heard the juices inside of me as they coated his long, fat finger. I suddenly felt his wet tongue on my clit while my finger was still moving in sync. He finally pushed my finger out of the way and sucked my clit into his warm mouth, sucking it softly and then harder. I felt dizzy and knew that I was about to cum.

"Suck this pussy, baby, and make it cum." He loved it when I talked shit and told him what to do to the pussy. "Suck this pussy, yes, yes." He pushed his finger into my pussy harder while he sucked and flicked his tongue over my swollen clit.

He came up for air, only long enough to say, "Give daddy this pussy, girl." I gripped his unbraided hair tightly between my fingers and fucked his face for another minute before I squirted my juices all over his finger and hand. When he pulled his finger out of me, he licked the cum off of me and said in a drunken state, "Damn, you taste so sweet. I could eat this pussy all day long."

I watched impatiently as he took off his clothes and revealed the most beautiful body I had ever seen. I loved the thuggish ways he possessed and could cum just from admiring him. I had never met another who turned me on this way. His dick was so long and hard, perfectly formed, and made just for me. His balls hung just right, like ornaments on Christmas Day, and made me want one inside my cheek. If only I could make it happen, I would leave them in my cheeks while his dick found my tonsils.

I sat up and pulled him into my mouth. I knew he was ready to fuck, but I just had to taste him first, because I couldn't let all that chocolatey goodness go to waste. I tasted his pre-cum on my tongue as I sucked on the head. My mouth fit so perfectly around him, like it was formed just for his dick. His deep voice penetrated the walls.

"Suck this dick like you mean it, baby. Show a nigga how much you missed it."

I removed my mouth and traced the head with my tongue while I gripped his balls with my other hand and massaged them extra hard. I then put him back in my mouth, and when his long dick hit my tonsils, I relaxed and deep throated him like a porn star.

"Mmm, shit."

I looked up and watched as he leaned his head back and moaned from the warmth of my mouth. He reached out and placed his hand on the back of my head, as if he was forcing me to suck all of it, but he knew that he never had to force me. Sucking his dick was like eating a rare delicacy, so expensive that only the richest of people could afford it.

Having his dick in my mouth was always a pleasure, and I truly enjoyed it. My only wish was hoping he wouldn't cum too quick so I could suck him longer, but the pressure of my lips always made him shoot quicker than I wanted him to. However, he's a gangsta and gives me nothing but thug love, which made him get hard back to back.

As he slid in and out of my mouth, I could see his wet dick glistening in the light, covered by my saliva. I let it fall all the way out of my mouth and told him hungrily, "Lay back on the couch and pull your legs up and spread them." I smiled seductively and continued, "Let me show you how a real bitch gets down."

Like the real man he was, he did just as I told him to. I got down on my knees in front of him and reached over to massage his balls before I flicked my tongue over them.

"Yeah, baby, do that shit."

His voice motivated me even more. I sucked one in my mouth at a time, lightly at first and then harder with each passing second.

"Oh shit," he said it so low I barely heard him.

I allowed saliva to drip from my mouth and drain down to his asshole, and then I took my finger and rubbed the saliva around his hole before I pushed my bird finger into him. He cut his eyes at me but said nothing. He hated when I did that shit but loved how it felt, so he never stopped me. I pulled my finger out and pushed it back in with greater force. One lone word escaped his sexy lips. "Fuck."

He flinched but still didn't stop me. I continued to fuck him as I put his dick back in my mouth. When I went all the way down on his dick, I slid my finger in and out and then slid it back in as I came up. I knew he was about cum because I felt his vein pulsing, but he told me anyway, "Oh shit, baby, I'm about to cum." I braced myself so I could catch all of his seeds.

I sucked him faster, steady fucking his asshole until I felt his warm juice hit the back of my throat. He was sweet yet salty at the same time. His creamy cum glided down my throat and coated my insides. "Mmm hmm," I moaned. And enjoyed his flavor. I loved his cum so much that I could drink a cup with every meal. I didn't stop until I had drained every single drop, and then I licked up and down his shaft, cleaning him up, my finger still inside of him. He was limp from our session, and I knew just what to do to get him back right.

"Be a good girl and come give daddy some of that pussy now," he stated with a smirk on his face while he slowly jacked his dick back to life.

Instead of doing what he said, I got up and sat on the opposite end of the couch. I spread my legs to where my pussy lips slightly parted with my clit poking out between them as if it was playing hide and seek. I smiled and asked, "Do you like what you see?"

He said nothing but continued to watch as I pinched my nipples and rolled them between my fingertips. I pushed a breast up to my lips and stuck my tongue out to meet it. I could feel my clit jump as I flicked my tongue over a nipple and then pulled it between my lips and sucked. I stopped only for a second and asked, "You wanna suck one too?"

I chuckled a little and then switched to the other breast, giving it the same amount of pleasure. "Do that shit, baby," he demanded, as he sat there and stroked his dick with a smirk across his beautiful yet hard face.

He started to get up, thinking that I was gonna let him do to me what I was already doing, but I shook my head no, saying, "I'm running this shit tonight and right now, I only want you to watch."

He smirked again and replied, "Damn, girl, you gonna do a nigga like that?"

I nodded and moved my hands from my nipples and went farther down, spreading my pussy lips, one lip with each hand, and my clit popped out from its hiding spot and bulged as if it was going to burst from all the pressure. "Ssss, yes." I pulled the hood back and rubbed a finger over the raw flesh that was exposed while letting out a slight moan, "Mmm."

I rubbed on it for a minute before sliding a finger down to my open hole, and pushed it inside, instantly coating it with my creamy cum. I had my eyes closed when I heard him say, "Damn, baby, come on, don't do me like that."

I opened my eyes and looked at him seductively before stating, "You want some of this pussy right now?" I pushed my finger in and then out a few times, and then pulled it all the way out and stuck it in my mouth. "Mmm, this pussy tastes so sweet," I told him seductively, and then continued, "No wonder you can't stay away." I then went back to playing with my clit and watched as his dick grew harder.

I jacked my clit as if it were a mini dick, until I felt a dizzying sensation. "Cum for daddy," he stated hungrily while watching me. I looked him in the eyes as my cum squirted out.

He shook his head and started getting up again, stating in a demanding voice, "I'm not waiting for this pussy any longer."

He looked at me angrily for making him wait on my goods, then he lifted my legs up and placed them over his shoulders, putting me in the buck position. My pussy opened for its owner, because his dick was what it craved. He licked his lips and then looked at me as the head of his dick found its home and slid in. My legs being all the way back allowed him to go deeper, but I wanted him drowning in it. "Oh, yes baby, go deeper. Fuck me deeper," I urged him between breaths, as his dick disappeared and reappeared.

The feeling of pain and pleasure at the same time had me drunk with emotion. His dick was so big, so thick, and so damn good, always making me feel as if it was my first time every time. I reached up and pinched his nipples hard as he slammed into me and asked, "Who does this pussy belong to?"

I didn't answer him, because he knew who owned it. Our skins clapped together, as if giving an applause for our show. His dick was so deep, I swore I could feel it in my chest. "Fuck me harder. Come on, baby, make this pussy cum for you," I demanded. His skin was covered in sweat, and little drops fell on me, as if it was lightly raining. My white, creamy cum covered his dick, as if it was icing on a chocolate cake. So succulent, so sweet, and so rich. "Faster, baby, fuck me faster."

He listened to my request and gained some speed as I watched his dick go in and out of me, his balls hitting my ass with each thrust. My breasts bounced around on my chest as if I was running a one-hundred-yard dash.

There it was once again, that feeling. That pulsing in the vein that runs the length of him, making it feel as if he were growing bigger right there inside of me. Like a seed planted in fertilizer with fresh water being poured over it and a little ray of sunshine lighting its path. Growing big and strong, only to be picked by an admirer and be displayed in a beautiful glass vase in the window for all the world to see.

He closed his eyes in ecstasy as his juices filled my insides, hitting my walls with his essence. His voice penetrated the walls, the same way his dick penetrated me. "I'm cumming, baby, I'm cumming."

He began to slow his thrusts one long stroke at a time, as I told him, "Fill me up, baby."

When he was empty, he didn't pull out, but instead, he lay on top of me with his dick still lodged within my walls. The sweat of our bodies caused our skin to mold together as if someone were sculpting us into a statue. We lie there, and I ran my fingers through his hair as we slowly caught our breath. Our eyes closed as time passed, and we drifted into peaceful slumber.

***

I felt his long, pointed tongue slide down the middle of my pussy lips. "Mmm, yes, baby," I whispered, but didn't want to open my eyes. I knew it wasn't a dream, because even in a dream nothing could have felt that good. "Oh god, yes." I cried out when he pushed a finger into my wet hole and placed his thumb over my clit. His hot breath sent a sensation to my asshole as my hips slowly rotated. "Oh, baby, it feels so damn good."

As his tongue found its way back to my swollen bud, he moved his thumb and placed it where his tongue was before. My early morning piss being held back put extra pressure inside my walls. As I reached down, putting both of my hands on the back of his head, I raised my legs up and spread them even farther.

I wanted him to be able to reach each and every fold of this pussy, his pussy. "That's right, lil' mama, open this pussy up for daddy," he told me, as he added another finger and turned into my ass at the same time.

I was afraid to cum because I didn't want it to be over, but I found it very hard to hold back anymore. I opened my eyes and watched as he flicked his tongue over my clit fast then slower. He sucked on it as if he were French kissing it. "Oh, baby, yes."

This nigga knew just what the fuck he was doing. I felt my heart speed up and knew that I wouldn't be able to hold it much longer. He came up long enough to demand, "Cum for me, baby. Squirt that shit right in my mouth."

At that very instant, I came. My moans got louder as my juices squirted out of me and onto his fingers and lips, coating his trimmed goatee. "Oh yes, yes, baby." Still, he kept sucking me oh so sweetly. I couldn't hold it anymore and felt my hot piss slowly begin to pour out, but still, he didn't stop. I felt it as it puddled beneath me, and I giggled and said, "That's why I love your nasty ass." The couch could be replaced, but the feelings he brought to my body couldn't be touched.

"Come on, girl, let's go get cleaned up," he stated as he grabbed my hand and pulled me up from the couch, leading me to the bathroom so we could immerse ourselves in a nice hot shower. He got in first and then helped me get in behind him.

My street thug, so hard and demanding in the streets, yet, so soft and submissive with me. I was able to see a side of him that no other ever would, and that kept me loyal and longing only for him and his touch. The water cascaded down and hit his beautiful dark skin, leading beads of water upon him, sticking to him as if they were afraid to let go. Looking like diamonds in the sun emitting a breathtaking shimmer and blinding you with their beauty.

I slightly closed my eyes as the water fell, and said, "I always look forward to this time with you."

He lovingly replied, "Don't worry, lil' mama, I'll always come back."

I got the washcloth and lathered it up and then pressed it against his skin, watching as the suds slid down his physique, some hanging from his nipples, trying to hold on like icicles on a roof's edge.

He leaned over and ran his tongue over my lips, and then sucked the bottom one into his mouth. He gently bit it as his hand found a nipple.

"Ssss, yes, baby." That's all I could manage to get out as he rolled a nipple between his finger and thumb. My nipples were so hard that they ached as he pulled and twisted, causing me to flinch at the pleasurable pain. He suddenly stopped and turned me around so that my back would be facing him, and then he reached around me with both arms and kidnapped them again, twisting them as if he was opening a jar.

I felt his hard dick pressing against the back of my thighs right under my ass cheeks, but I knew him well enough to know that he would take his time giving it to me the way I wanted. As his dick slid through the middle of my thighs and brushed against my clit, he teasingly asked, "You want some of this dick?"

I greedily replied "Yes, oh yes, please. Fuck me and give that good dick."

His teasing continued, "Nah, not yet. I want you to beg for this dick." He pushed it back and forth as it lightly brushed my clit, all the while still playing with my nipples. "Beg for this dick. Tell me how bad you want it."

I felt his breath on my neck as he continued to tease me. "Please fuck me, please give it to me, baby. I need you inside of me."

He removed a hand from my nipple and grabbed my wet hair, pulling it until my face turned and met his eyes, and then we kissed. Our kiss was explosive and full of passion, until he broke away and pushed my head forward. He bent me over and spread my ass cheeks enough to gain access, and my pussy opened voluntarily, anticipating his arrival.

"You asked for this dick, so I'm gonna give it to you, and you better make this shit cum."

His dick slid in hard and fast, and then he pulled it out slowly all the way to the head and slammed it back into me, forcefully repeating this move several times. "Oh god, yes, fuck this pussy."

I reached down and began pulling and twisting my clit. He started to speed up and demanded, "Take this dick, baby. Take this shit like a good girl. Make this dick cum."

I held my other hand flat against the wall to help my balance and to keep my head from hitting it. My other hand was still masturbating my clit as I got closer to an orgasm. He loved it when I told him I was going to cum, so I always expressed it to him. "Shit, I'm about to cum."

He fucked me even harder as my cum coated his dick while some slid down my inner thighs. "That's right, cum for me, lil' mama. Coat this dick with that shit."

After his dick was covered with cum, he pulled it all the way out and then rammed it into my ass. "Ugh," I grunted from the sudden impact.

When he pulled it back out, he pushed back in slower, one delicious inch at a time. Once he had all of it inside of me again, he slapped my ass cheeks and caused a stinging sensation. Our bodies collided, splashing water in between us.

Holding both of my palms against the wall, now I took the full length of his dick. "Yes, baby, fuck me." It felt as if he was getting bigger, so I knew I was about to cum. I egged him on by saying, "Cum for me, daddy, cum all on this ass."

After a few more thrusts, he pulled out and shot his dick cream all over my ass cheeks, and then he took his dick in his hand and spanked me with it. His thug love always took me to levels I never knew existed.

When we were done, we finished our shower by bathing ourselves and then each other, having the time of our lives, tickling and teasing each other. When we were done splashing around in the water, we got out and dried each other off. I lotioned my body down with Victoria's Secret lotion, and as the aroma filled the air, he grabbed my chin and pulled my face up toward him and kissed the tip of my nose. His romantic gestures stayed close to my heart, because I knew the world would never see this side of him.

When we walked into the bedroom, he put on some boxers and lay down on the bed. I grabbed his T-shirt and slid it over my head before lying down beside him. When he turned on his right side, I snuggled up next to him with my back against his chest as he threw his arm around me. Before we fell asleep, he made sure to tell me, "You know when I leave I'm gonna always come back to you." He lightly kissed my shoulder before continuing, "Don't ever worry about that, baby. I'll always be back."

I took a second before responding, "I know, baby, I know."

***

The doorbell woke me from my slumber, and I was so comfortable in his embrace that I almost didn't get up, thinking perhaps they would go away. But whoever was at the door was very persistent, because the doorbell rang again. The sound of it didn't disturb him, so he continued to snooze. "This better be good," I said to myself as I lifted his arm from around me.

He stirred a little before rolling over on his back and lightly snoring. I glanced down and admired his girth that was hiding under the sheet, or at least attempting to. It was too big to try and take cover, and his early morning hardness seemed longer than the night before. I smiled and then reached down and brushed my nails over it before getting out of bed.

The doorbell rang once again before I could make it all the way to it. "Okay, okay, damn. Who the fuck is it?" I asked in an irritated voice before pulling it open and seeing my best friend, who also happened to be my only friend. As soon as I saw her, I said, "Girl, you was about to get cussed the fuck out."

She replied, "Sorry, but a bitch is bored and didn't have shit else to do. So, here I am." She went and sat on the couch and then asked, "What are you up to today?"

I smiled before I replied, "Girl, I was about to ride some dick. You wanna join me?" I had never thought about sharing the gift between his legs, but I decided that I was going to give him something special.

She jumped up from the couch and smiled, saying, "Now you know I'm not turning down no dick."

I grabbed her hand and walked her to the bedroom where he was just opening his eyes and getting ready to start his day. When we walked in, a confused look crossed his face, and before he could get a word out, I placed a lone finger over his lips. "Shh, just relax, baby. I got a little something special for you today." I pulled his T-shirt off me and then turned to her and said, "Get undressed. It's time to fuck."

She got undressed and said, "Well then, bitch, let's fuck."

I started by kissing her and pulled gently on her nipples with my fingers. I then put my lips upon them and gently sucked. I could hear my nigga in the background, "Damn, baby, you fuckin' me up with that shit."

I gently bit her nipple, making her flinch from surprise, and when she put her hand on the back of my head, I heard her moan, "Mmm, yes." I took one of my fingers and found her clit that was already hard and poking out from between her fat, shaved pussy lips. I moved my finger on it in a back and forth motion and pressed hard at the same time. I heard her say, "Oh my god, this feels so good."

I cut my eyes over to the bed and saw him rubbing his dick through the sheet, so I said to him, "You liking this shit, ain't you, daddy?"

He smiled at me and replied, "I like everything you do, baby. Everything."

I dropped to my knees, and when she spread her legs, I took my fingers and spread her pussy lips. I made sure he had a good view when I stuck my tongue out and began flicking it over her swollen clit. "Oh my god, yes."

Her saying that only motivated me even more. I took a finger and glided it inside of her wet pussy and pulled it in and out a few times before adding another one. Her pussy gripped my fingers as I pulled them out and then pushed them back in. She thrusted her hips hard as I sucked on her swollen clit, telling me, "Shit, you 'bout to make me cum. Don't stop, I'm cumming."

I continued to suck on her clit while her cum coated my fingers. When she finished cumming, I grabbed her hand and guided her to the bed. "Come on, we ain't done." I pulled the sheet back from over my man's perfectly sculpted dick, and then we climbed onto the bed with him. "Spread your legs like a bitch likes you to do. I got a special treat for you."

He spread his legs like I told him, giving me easy access to his balls. My friend looked at them as I told her, "Come on, girl. There's enough to go around."

I took his left into my mouth while she bent down and pulled the right one into hers. "Holy shit." That's all he managed to get out when he felt the sensation of both of his balls being sucked. After a few minutes, we released his balls from our mouths, leaving them wet with saliva, and then we started kissing again.

I knew that he was enjoying the show, but he also knew that this may never happen again. I was greedy with all the good dick he carried around. I cut my eyes up at him just in time to hear him speak, "Damn, baby, what's up? You gonna leave a nigga hanging?"

We stopped kissing, and then we both started licking the head of his dick, making sure to get the pre-cum that had formed. I pulled him into my mouth and went all the way down to the base before coming back up. When I released him, she swallowed him next. "Mmm, hmm, suck that shit," he moaned, as we took turns sucking his massive member.

He pulled his legs all the way up, bending his knees, and as he did, we each grabbed an ass check and exposed his tight asshole. "Fuck." That's all he managed to say before both of our tongues were licking his hole.

I came up long enough to tell him, "You better not cum," and then I stuck not one but two fingers into him, knowing I would pay for it later. In and out, I fucked him while we sucked on his balls again.

I felt a finger brushing across my nipple and looked up, noticing he was brushing hers too. I felt a little jealous but let it pass, because all of this was my fault. I heard him as he spoke to me, "Come put that pussy on this dick. You fuckin' me up right now." As I pulled my fingers out of him, he stretched his legs out to full capacity. "Get on this dick, baby."

I smiled and turned my back to him so that I could sit on him reverse style. "You want this pussy, daddy?" I only let the head go inside of me, teasing him and talking shit to him at the same time. "Answer me, nigga. You want this pussy?"

"Damn right. Give me that shit and quit fucking playing," he demanded as he grabbed my hips and pulled me down, making his dick disappear inside of me.

I said to my friend, "Suck my clit while I ride this dick." My friend happily obliged and pulled my clit into her mouth. Using my feet as leverage, I pushed myself up and then slowly went back down, all the while holding the back of her head so her rhythm didn't stop. "Oh yes, yes. This feels so good."

My clit pulsed from the pressure of her tongue and lips, and I knew that I was about to cum. I started riding him faster as he steadily held my hips. "Cum for me. Cum on daddy's dick," he said to me.

I hollered out, "Shit, I'm cumming. I'm fucking cumming."

I could feel him pulsating inside of me when he said, "Damn, girl, I'm cumming with you."

I felt his hot liquid fill my insides, coating my walls. As I slowed down, my friend came up off my clit, leaving it numb. Once I was filled with his sweetness, I let him fall out of me. We all breathed heavily, anticipating our next move.

I told my friend, "Turn around and get doggy style, it's your turn." She did as I asked while my man looked at me funny. I said to him, "It's okay, boo. I want you to have a good time."

When she turned around and spread her ass cheeks, I started jacking his dick so he would get back hard. He shoved

21

a finger in her pussy, and as always, he began to grow. He looked at me again and asked, "Are you sure about this?"

I smiled at his respect and told him, "Fuck that pussy, baby, and you better fuck good." I guided his dick to her open hole, and as he entered her, I moved my hand from around him. I then went and lay down in front of her so she could eat his cum from out of me. As he fucked her, she licked down the length of my pussy lips and then stuck her tongue into my open hole to taste the essence that he had left behind. "Oooh, yeah, suck it," I told her as she came up and sucked my clit between her lips.

I could hear his body slamming into her. He held her ass cheeks and fucked her so hard, he grunted, "Ugh, ugh." He fucked her as if she violated a code of the streets. She did violate, but it was me who made her, and I couldn't wait until he punished me for it.

He slapped her ass cheek with a greater force than he had ever done to me, and it caused me to look up. I could see in his eyes that he was going to cum, so I pushed her from between my legs. I said to him, "Hold on, baby, I'm coming."

I got up and went to him and pulled him back so he would fall out of her. I then took his dick in my hand and gently stroked it as she got up and turned to us. I held onto it as she took it into her mouth. I began kissing him as his cum shot down her throat and she swallowed. He slapped me on my ass cheek and stated, "Thank you, but you know you're going to pay for this."

I kissed him gently on his bottom lip and said, "I just wanted to do something special for you."

He smiled and said, "You didn't have to, you're special enough."

He got off the bed and went into the bathroom and turned the shower water on. Steam came out of the bathroom door that he had left open. I turned to my friend and said, "Come on, let's go get cleaned up." She followed me into the spare bathroom so we could take a shower. We giggled as we lathered each other up, paying close attention to each other's clits. "I guess one more session won't hurt us," I said as the hot water hit our bodies.

We lay down in the bottom of the tub in the sixty-nine position. I sucked her clit into my mouth as she did the same to mine. Her pussy was sweet and tasted so good. "You been holding back from a bitch."

She didn't answer because she was so focused on what she was doing to me. I had never imagined us being here like this. We had been friends since middle school, and this was something we had never talked about. I had a small shelf attached to the shower wall where I stored my toys. I reached up and pulled a small vibrator off of it. I said to her, "Hold on, I got something for this good pussy of yours."

She smiled and said, "Go ahead and give me what you got," and then she pulled my clit back into her mouth.

I guided the vibrator into her pussy and turned it on while moving it in and out of her. "Mmm, mmm, hmm," she moaned loudly while still sucking my pearl. I noticed her creamy juice coating the vibrator, and then pulled it out and slid into her ass. She finally let my clit go and said, "That shit feel so good, mmm, mmm." I knew she was about to cum before she even said it. "Oh my god, I'm cumming. I'm fucking cumming."

As her cum squirted out, I took my tongue and caught as much as I could, and as she pulled my clit back between her lips, I came too.

We finally got up and showered off, and then I asked her, "Did you have a good time?"

She giggled and replied, "Girl, you didn't even have to ask me that. I had a wonderful time, thank you."

I told her, "That's what friends are for."

We got out and walked back to the bedroom so she could get her clothes and get dressed. I went in search of my thug but couldn't find him. I knew in my heart that he had already left. The streets were calling for him. However, I knew that he would be back. He always came back to me. He knew that this pussy was his home and the door stayed open just for him. No one else would ever live here.

I threw on his T-shirt and a pair of his boxers. No panties, no bra. Just his belongings against my naked flesh. I walked her to the door and told her before she left, "Call me so we can hang out."

She hugged me and said, "Oh, I'll definitely call. Thanks again for the good time."

I shut the door and I was all alone once again. Just me, my thoughts, and his aroma. He was so intoxicating, and I was addicted to him like a drug. I got pleasure just from the mere thought of him, and if I thought about him too long, I would become wet and cum on myself. He was my thug, my man, my only desire.

I sat down on the couch and turned on the television, but I couldn't concentrate. My thoughts took me to earlier, and I felt myself getting wet. I lay back and propped my legs up once again. Maybe if I replayed where I started off at yesterday, he would show back up and we could do it all again.

I slid my hand through the hole of the boxer shorts I had on and found my clit. I moaned to myself as I pressed down and did small circular motions on top of it. "Mmm, mmm," I moaned and imagined that he was sitting there in front of me, his dick in his hand, watching me play with my wet pussy. I slid my finger down my slit until I reached my hole and pushed the tip inside. I went in and out a few times before pulling it out, and then I stuck it in my mouth and sucked my juices off of it. I sucked on it like it was a dick instead. I then stuck it back inside, doing the circular motions over again, but I went harder and faster.

I was about to cum, so I took my other hand and pinched a nipple really hard through the fabric of the T-shirt. I called his name as the wetness erupted and gushed out of me like a wave in the ocean. My heart beat faster, as if it were trying to leap out of my chest. I began to slow my rhythm until I was completely done, and when I opened my eyes, he was there again, sitting on the coffee table in front of me, dick in hand, ready to come back home.

Sugar E. Walls

Chapter Two

Beyond the Pole

As the coldness of the round steel pole slid between my ass cheeks, my heart began to beat faster. "This is what it sounds like when doves cry." The music was blaring and the voice of Prince flowed from the speakers. I was dancing to the beat of my own drum. The drum that pulsed between my pussy lips. My thong was soaking wet and my pussy juice left them sticky. When I pulled the skimpy top off that I had on, my nipples stood erect.

"Woo hoo."

"Yeah, take that shit off."

The men in the crowd shouted and went crazy, but at that moment, pleasing them was the farthest thing from my mind. I grabbed my breasts, and as I twisted my perky nipples, I tugged on them lightly. "Mmm, yes," I moaned loudly, although I knew that no one else could hear me.

I may have been dancing in an overcrowded strip club, but in my mind, I was all alone. I pushed one of my breasts up to my mouth and licked my hardened nipple. "Maybe I'm just too demanding, maybe I'm just like my mother. She's never satisfied." The music continued playing as I pulled my wet thong to the side, and when I slid a finger into my dripping hole, I could hear the crowd, but I was too far gone in my own zone to pick it up. All I could think about right at that moment was making my pussy cum, and I wouldn't stop until I got what I wanted.

When I pulled my wet finger out and placed it on my swollen clit, I opened my eyes. I looked around at all those men watching me masturbate, and it had me hypnotized. I pressed and massaged my clit until a dizzying feeling came over me. It only took a minute for me to reach my limit. Right then and right there on that very stage, I had begun to cum for all who were there to see. "Yes, sss, yes," I said as my juices squirted out.

After cumming, I rubbed my glistening juices all over my stomach and then my nipples. I coated them as if I had rubbed myself down with lotion. When I stuck my fingers in my mouth to suck off the leftover cum, the music suddenly stopped. I looked like a deer caught in headlights. "Oh shit," I stated as I looked out at the crowd, and then ran off the stage and left all the money behind.

"Girl, what the fuck was that?" one of the other dancers named Cookie asked when I walked back in the dressing room.

I sat down at my station and responded, "Bitch, my ass was horny as fuck. I needed to cum."

She laughed and shook her head before walking out to go do her set. I got up to get out of my wet thong and heard the door open. I looked up and saw the finest man I had ever seen, and as he spoke, my pussy became wet again. "You left all of this on the stage." He looked me up and down before continuing, "Just thought I'd bring it to you."

He was holding a small clear bag stuffed with bills. So many that I wondered if the men out there had any more to give the other dancers. I looked from the fine specimen to the bag and licked my lips before I said, "Thank you, I don't know what came over me out there."

I walked closer to him, as my nipples pointed the way, so I could retrieve my earnings, and as I reached for the bag, he said, "You know, I could help you out with your little issue." His smile melted my soul and made me feel weak. I was usually a bold bitch, but there was something about him that caused me to be submissive. I didn't even know this black god in front of me, but at that moment, it didn't even matter.

The bag of money fell from his grip as I reached out and unzipped his jeans. I pulled them down all the way to his ankles, and as he stepped out of them, he said, "Let me give that pussy what it really needs." He was so demanding and his aura had my insides screaming. It felt like an inferno had been lit inside of me, and only his cum could extinguish it. His dick stood straight out like a gun pointing at its victim, and I couldn't wait for his pistol to shoot me.

I wrapped my small hand around him as I looked into his eyes, and said, "I hope you know how to use this thing."

I smiled and dropped to my knees so I could taste a sample. It was long and thick, and the pre-cum on the tip shined like a diamond in the light. I stuck my tongue out and used the pointed tip of it to lick the sticky substance off. As the head disappeared between my lips, he grabbed the back of my head and said, "Yeah, girl, suck this dick. Damn, that shit feels good." I went slowly down his length, and as it touched the back of my throat, I relaxed my gag reflexes. I swallowed his dick with ease and felt him grip my head tighter. His moans made me suck harder. "Mmm hmm, yes, shit yeah."

Slow and then fast, but never letting up on my grip. "Slurp, slurp, slurp." The wet sounds that came from my mouth had me on edge. Only the pulse of him slowed me down, because I wasn't ready for him to cum. I wanted his dick inside of me, beating my walls down. I loved to be fucked hard and fast, and it had been a while.

I let his dick fall out of my mouth, and then he asked, "What's up, shawty? Why you stopped?"

I didn't answer him, but instead, I walked away from him and went to my dressing table. When I got there, I leaned over in my chair and reached around to spread my ass cheeks open.

I said in a hungry voice, "Come on, daddy. Come show this pussy what you got."

He walked up behind me and slapped my ass with his stiff dick. The stinging sensation made me flinch and say, "Yes, mmm, hmm." I then felt a finger enter my pussy, and as he slid it in and out, I told him, "Stop teasing me and give me some dick."

He pulled his finger out, and then I felt the head of his dick at my wet opening. As his thumb found my asshole and entered, he slid deep inside of me. My pussy sounded like wet macaroni being stirred and turned me on even more. Listening to our bodies collide was like sweet music to my ears. He slapped my ass and said, "Throw that pussy back, girl." I did as he said, "Yeah, that's it. Throw that pussy." I reached one of my hands down between my legs and played with my clit as he fucked me just like I wanted.

All of a sudden, the door opened and a voice said, "Damn, I came back just in time." Cookie was a cool ass bitch and wild as fuck.

The man behind me never broke his rhythm as she walked up behind him and got on her knees. She spread his ass cheeks and ran her tongue the length of his ass crack. "Oh shit," was all I heard him say. When she reached between his legs and gripped his balls, I felt him squeeze my ass tighter. I knew that I would have red welts when this was over, but they would be well earned. I almost lost my breath as he pumped into me faster. He said, "I'm about to cum."

Cookie got up from her knees and told him, "Pull that dick out so I can drink that shit up." He pulled his dick out of me, and she grabbed it just in time to swallow his cum. I watched as his dick disappeared down her throat, and it actually made me a little envious. I bent down and cupped his balls in my hand. I could see his legs shake and start to get weak, knowing he had reached his limit. When he became soft, she let him fall out of her mouth and then turned to kiss me. I obliged and kissed her back, tasting his salty juice inside her mouth. We stopped kissing, and Cookie said, "We should really hook up some time." I smiled and agreed before standing up and getting myself together. It had been a long night, and I was ready to go home and curl up in the bed.

It was breezy when I walked outside, and as the wind blew across my chest, my nipples reacted and stood at attention. I thought maybe I should ask Cookie to come home with me tonight, because having a warm body next to me sounded like a great idea. I turned around and went back inside so I could invite her over to stay the night. I loved a big dick going inside of me, but tonight I wanted something a little softer.

I found Cookie still in the dressing room, sitting in front of her mirror admiring her perfectly round nipples. The darkness of her areolas made the rest of her skin glow. When she looked up and noticed me staring at her, she began to put on a show and said, "I had a lot of fun earlier. You ready to do it again?"

As I walked up behind her and looked at her through the mirror, I reached around and pulled hard on her right nipple, and said, "You wanna come home with me tonight and have an even better time?"

She thought for only a brief second before answering, "Hmm, I'd love to get deep in that pussy before closing my eyes." She then stood up out of her chair and pinched both of her nipples before sticking her tongue out and rolling it over them one at a time. I couldn't help myself as I leaned down and met my tongue with hers. Her nipples were the size of freshly picked raspberries, so firm and oh so sweet. I pulled one in between my lips as she grabbed the back of my head and pushed. Still barely dressed from her set on stage didn't leave much to remove. I cut my eyes up at her as she moaned from the pressure of my mouth, "Mmm, mm, yes." I reached a hand down and pushed it between her thighs. Her white thongs were wet and sticky as I rubbed my hand over them. "Yes, that feels so good. Mmm hmm," she stated as she enjoyed my touch.

I came up from her nipple and began kissing her open mouth. I shoved my tongue inside and explored the newfound territory. I pulled back and said, "I want to taste that pussy right now."

She smiled and then hopped up on her makeup stand. When she pulled her legs up and spread them, I pulled her thong to the side. Her clit was fat and swollen and peeked out from her pussy slit. "This pussy is fat, ain't it?" she asked seductively, as I gently flicked a finger over her protruding clit.

She reached her hand over and pulled a long pink dildo out of her bag. She ran it down her length and then slid it slowly inside of her. When she pulled it out, it was shimmery from her juices. As she started to push it back in, I pulled her hand up and pulled the dildo in between my lips, sucking her juices off of it. When I let her hand go, she pushed the toy back inside of her.

As she filled her pussy walls, I bent over and sucked her clit into my mouth. I sucked it hard like it was a straw in a milkshake, as she called out, "Oh fuck, I'm gonna cum all over this dick. Yes, oh yes. Fuck, I'm cumming."

As her cum squirted, I kept sucking her clit, and when she pulled the dildo out of her, I pushed my tongue into her hole. She trembled at the feeling I gave, and the more her legs shook the deeper my tongue went.

I finally came up for air, and we looked at each other and giggled. I didn't know what was so funny, but neither of us could stop laughing. As she put her legs down, I backed up some so she could have room to get herself together. I couldn't wait for her to stick some dick up inside of me, so I rushed her to put something on so we could leave. I was ready to get the fuck outta there and into bed. She slid a sheer dress over her and gathered her things, and then said, "I'm ready now."

As we walked together past the club goers, all heads turned toward us. Cookie intentionally lifted her short dress up and ran a finger over her clit, and then licked the tip of it. She was such a nasty bitch, and that shit made me crazy. I thought about picking one of the fine ass men that was there and bringing them with us, but decided against it. I was pretty sure that Cookie was going to strap up and perform just as good as them. The bouncer at the front door nodded at us and smiled while he said, "Dayum, sure would like to tag along on that ride."

Cookie told him in response, "Nah, baby, you ain't gonna sling that dick like I'm going to. So, maybe next time around." She then took a hand and put it on the front of his pants and squeezed his dick as she stood on her tippy toes and licked across his lips, leaving them coated with her saliva. I couldn't wait to get this bitch to my apartment to see just what she was going to do to me.

When we got to the parking lot, we decided that we would take my car and she would take a cab back to the club the next day to pick hers up. I told her, "I can drive you back. You don't have to catch a cab."

She laughed and said, "Nah, when I'm done, you won't have the energy to drive me back." This bitch talked a good game, and I hoped she could back it up once she put that strap on.

Instead of going around to the passenger side to get in, she climbed across the driver's seat and middle console, her fat pussy lips showing as she made her move. I didn't have to feel her wetness because I could see it shimmering at her hole. My mouth watered thinking about licking it off of her, but I maintained my control.

Cookie spread her legs and masturbated her clit on the drive there. Every time she came, she would rub her fingers in it and then put it on my mouth so I could taste it. I finally told her, "Damn, I ain't never seen a bitch cum so much."

She cut her eyes at me and said, "Girl, this pussy could cum all day and never get tired."

My clit was throbbing so hard that it felt like it was about to burst. I sped up because I was now even more ready than ever and wanted to get there quick. All of a sudden, out of nowhere, I saw flashing lights behind me. "Oh, fuck, there's a cop behind me. Fix yourself because I gotta pull over," I said to Cookie in a distressed manner.

She reached over and pinched my cheek, and then said, "Pull on a side street and let me handle this." I started to protest but thought better of it. I knew there was power in the pussy, and Cookie knew just how to use that power to control any situation.

I pulled over on a dimly lit side street and shut the car off as Cookie lifted up one leg and propped it on the dashboard. I shook my head and giggled as the officer approached my side of the car. I rolled my window down as he asked, "Excuse me, miss, do you know how fast you were going?"

I looked up at him to answer, but before I got a chance to speak, Cookie took control. "Oh, sir, you have to excuse her. She was rushing to get us home so she could stick her tongue in this wet ass pussy I've been teasing her with."

The officer bent down and looked over at her just in time to see her slide two fingers inside of her pussy. His eyes got big as he stuttered, "Um, uh, uh. I-I'm sorry, but... How 'bout

I just—I'm just gonna give you a warning and let you go this time."

Cookie cut him off and said, "Too bad you're on shift. You probably could have joined us. A little dick never hurt anybody."

He then said, while passing me a card with his number on it, "Yeah, um, here, take my card in case of an emergency. You ladies have a good night." When he walked away from the car, we bust out laughing. I could not believe Cookie said that shit, but was so glad that I didn't have to pay for a speeding ticket and get points against my license.

I turned around in the street after the officer drove off, and headed to my apartment. The way Cookie played that scene made me even more turned on. "Cookie, you crazy as hell, bitch," I said to her as I put my key into the lock of my apartment door.

She reached up and pinched one of my nipples and said, "Not as crazy as I'm about to make you when I suck that cum out of your pussy." I just shook my head and opened the door, and as soon as Cookie walked inside, she pulled her little dress off and turned toward me and said, "Get undressed, bitch. I'm so ready to fuck."

She then turned to the couch and went and sat on it. I got undressed and walked over to her and said, "Come on, let's go to the bedroom." I grabbed her hand and pulled her up from the couch and walked her to my bedroom.

As soon as we walked in it, she went to the bed and told me, "Come on. Get doggy style. I got a special treat for you." I did as she said, and my heart started beating faster, anticipating what she had in store for me.

Cookie got behind me and licked from the top of my ass crack to my pussy hole. She came back up a little and circled my asshole with the tip of her tongue as I felt a finger go into my pussy. She sucked and licked my asshole so good I thought I would go into cardiac arrest. "Oh my god, Cookie. That shit feels so damn good. Mmm, hmm, yes, Cookie," I said as my forehead broke out into a sweat.

My heart beat extra fast as I reached down and squeezed my clit between my forefinger and thumb, pressing as hard as I could. The pressure was intense, and it only took a second for my cum to squirt out and hit Cookie right in the chin. I wondered when she was going to strap up and give me some dick, so I asked her, "Damn, Cookie, that shit feels good and all, but I'm a dick dyke and need something inside of me."

She came up from what she was doing and stated, "I got you, girl, you gon' get some dick." She then got off the bed and went to her bag and pulled out a nice-sized strap-on dick, and then stuck the silicone length into my mouth. As I enjoyed the fake dick going down to my throat, I stuck a finger inside of her. She was wet and slippery and moaned at the pleasure I was giving her, "Mmm, yeah."

I was ready for the fake dick to go up inside of me, so I let it fall out of my mouth and looked up at Cookie, saying, "Bitch, I'm ready for you to put this thing up inside of me," I got up and got on all fours with my ass up in the air. She came up on the bed, and when she spread my ass cheeks, she slid the strap-on into my open pussy. "Come on, Cookie, I want you to beat this pussy up. I like to be fucked hard," I said to her as she squeezed my ass cheeks and fucked me like a man.

"This hard enough for you? Huh, this dick hard enough for you?" she asked as she slammed into me.

"Yes, Cookie, yes. That's how I like this pussy to be fucked," I said as she slowed down and then sped back up again. "Bitch, I'm cumming, fuck. Yes, Cookie, I'm cumming," I hollered out as my pussy walls pushed out a waterfall.

She slowed down again and said, "Cum for me, that's right. Damn, I'm cumming too."

After we both came, she pulled the dick out of me and then reached for the phone. I asked her with a puzzled look, "Who are you calling?"

She smiled at me and said, "I'm calling for some real dick to come over to this motherfucker. Silicone ain't gonna do it for me tonight." She dialed and said to the person on the other end, "There's some pussy over here in violation that needs severe punishment." She cut her eyes at me, and then continued, "I need crime stoppers over here to save the day."

I knew then that she had called the officer from earlier, and just shook my head. She rambled off my address and hung up. About fifteen minutes later, I heard my doorbell ring. Cookie got up ass naked, and said while rushing to the door, "I'll get it." However, I still got up and followed behind her. When she opened the door, the officer from earlier stepped inside. Cookie put her hand on his chest and stopped him before he came all the way in. "Uh, uh, nigga. Take that shit off," she said in a demanding voice.

He looked from her to me and then up and down our naked bodies. We had both come to the door without anything on. He lifted his eyebrows and said, "That ain't no problem at all, ladies."

As he began undressing, Cookie got behind me and reached her arms around to my breasts. She took her fingers and started pinching my nipples, and then said, "Wanna suck one of these?"

His dick was nice and long and stood straight out like an arrow about to be shot out of a bow. He bent down and circled his tongue over one of my hardened nipples. I flinched and moaned, "Mmm hmm. That feels so good."

When he stood back up, we each grabbed a hand and pulled him to the couch. As soon as he sat down, we pushed his legs open. Cookie told him, "Just sit back and relax, 'cause we about to rape this dick." We both got on our knees and pulled a nut into our mouth.

"Holy shit." That's all he managed to get out as we sucked his nut sack. He grabbed a hold of his dick and slowly jacked it as we sucked him into an orgasm. When his cum shot out, we came up and licked it off of him.

I knew that I was going to have to get the seats of my couch cleaned professionally after this, so I told him, "Nigga, this dick better be worth it."

"Man, it's time for some real freaky shit," Cookie said, as she got up and cleared the coffee table that was in front of the couch. She positioned herself on it doggy style and said, "Come on and suck this ass for me."

The officer made no complaints as he leaned forward and stuck his tongue into her asshole. I went and stood in front of her and spread my pussy lips, begging her to suck it. "Please, suck this pussy, Cookie." If I would have known that Cookie could suck pussy that good, I would have been invited her over. I had never even thought about her in a sexual manner until tonight.

As she attacked my clit, I could hear the officer making slurping sounds on her asshole. I grinded my hips as Cookie sucked my clit hard. I could feel myself getting dizzy from the grip of her mouth on my pearl. "Oh shit, Cookie. Bitch, I'm cumming. Ooh, yes." No sooner than I said it, my cum squirted out and down the middle of my thighs, leaving a sticky essence behind.

The officer stood up and told Cookie, "Get ready, 'cause I'm about to put some pipe up in this ass."

And as he slid the head of his dick into her, she cried out, "That's right, fuck this ass, nigga. I love this shit."

I leaned over the back of her and put one hand on each ass cheek, spreading it wider for him. Watching his dick go in and out of her gave me a rush. He looked down at me and said, "Damn, this bitch got some good ass. Shit 'bout to make me cum." He then started pumping faster, and when he pulled his dick all the way out, he shot his cum right in my face. I rubbed it in with one hand and then licked off my fingers. The sticky liquid clung to my skin as a light breeze brushed across it, sending a coolness my body needed.

Cookie got up and said in a satisfied voice, "Damn, nigga, that's some good dick you got carrying around." Then she turned to me and stated, "Girl, you better hop on that dick before I get greedy with it."

I pushed the officer back on the couch as he wrapped a hand around his dick, getting it ready for me. I turned my back to him, spread my ass cheeks, and sat on the dick backward. I felt chills run down my spine as the head of his dick opened me up. I could feel the pressure way up in my chest. As I slid further down onto his goodness, I grabbed my nipples and pinched them hard enough to hurt. My pain mixed with his pleasure was amazing. Once he was all the way inside of me, I called out, "Oh my god, Cookie, you are so right. This dick feels so good."

He put his arms up behind his head and said, "That's right, ride this dick, girl. Fuck this dick like it's the last one you'll ever ride."

He sucked his bottom lip between his teeth as I slowly glided up and down on his manhood. Cookie positioned herself in front of me and pulled my aching clit into her mouth as I rode myself into an orgasm. "I'm cumming, yes, oh shit. This pussy about to cum all over this dick."

The officer behind me said, "Cum for me, cum for this dick, yeah."

I rode him faster as Cookie jerked my clit, and I felt like I was about to faint from the sudden rush of my orgasm. "Ooh, yes, yes," I hollered out as cum squirted out of me.

The officer then grabbed my hips and continued pushing his pelvis up, slamming his dick inside of me. It only took him a few more strokes before he said, "This dick is about to cum. Get up and swallow this shit." I jumped up off of him, and we both attacked his essence. I sucked the head of his dick as Cookie licked his shaft and massaged his balls. I swallowed hard as his cum shot down my throat.

Suddenly, the officer's pager went off, and although I was secretly hoping he wouldn't check it, he did anyway. I was disappointed when he said, "Sorry, ladies, but I gotta go. I gotta check out a situation going on as we speak. Thanks for the good time." He paused and then added, "And for the good pussy." He got up and got dressed without even bothering to clean his dick off. Before he walked out the door, he turned and said, "Make sure y'all call me. I'll always make time to come over." He smiled at us and then shut the door behind him.

Cookie and I decided to get some rest. We both had sets to do at the club later and wanted to be prepared. It felt kinda strange sleeping in my bed with another woman beside me. It had been so long since I shared that private space with anyone, but it did feel nice.

A sudden motion woke me from my slumber, and when I opened my eyes, I saw Cookie lying beside me with her legs spread wide and masturbating. I said to her in a groggy voice, "Damn, bitch, you could have woke me up to take care of that."

She let out a slight moan and said hungrily, "Mmm, it's never too late to join." I rolled over on my side and pushed her hand out of the way. I sucked on a nipple as I pressed and massaged her swollen clit. "Ah, yes, that shit feels good as fuck," she said as I moved my finger from her clit and slid it between her pussy lips, down to her dripping wet hole. She pushed her hips up as I guided two fingers inside of her and fucked her pussy. "Yes, girl, fuck this pussy. Make this pussy cum for you," she hollered as I repositioned myself between her legs, never removing my fingers. She grabbed a handful of my hair as I sucked her clit into my mouth. "Ssss, yeah. Oh yeah, suck it." I sucked her clit with as much pressure as my mouth could muster, until I heard those words, "Fuck, I'm cumming, don't stop, I'm fucking cumming." I sucked faster and harder as she continued to holler, "Aah, oh my god, oh my god, yes. Aah, fuck." And then she came all over my fingers.

The spot beneath her was now soaked from her juices. I finally let her clit go, and looked up at her and said, "You liked that shit, huh?" She smiled at me, and we laughed and then got up to go take a shower so we could get to the dance club where her car was still parked.

We had decided that tonight we would put on a real show for the customers coming to the club. Their hard-earned money would be well spent tonight, and we would definitely earn every single dollar. While in our dressing room getting ready for our set, we heard a knock on the door. "Come on in, it's open," I said while pulling up a thong that was way too small for my ass. My fat pussy lips protruded from the sides of the crotch, but my nasty ass wore them anyway. They would surely serve their purpose.

The owner of the club opened the door and walked in, saying, "You ladies about ready to go show the fuck out?" He smiled while at the same time, looking us up and down,

Cookie was the first to respond to him. "I don't know, why don't you come over here and inspect this pussy and see if it's ready?" She lifted a leg up and pulled her pussy lips apart while smiling at him seductively.

I shook my head at her boldness, but played along. "Yeah, why don't you inspect that fat pussy and make sure your customers are getting what they paid for," I said as I walked over to him and unzipped his zipper. He made no protest as I reached in his pants and pulled his monster out of its cave. "That's a really big dick you have there," I said as I ran my finger over it, then to my lips and licked the sticky juice off.

"Damn." That's all that he managed to get out before I was on my knees licking the head of his dick. I traced the line of the head with the tip of my tongue and then covered it completely with my mouth. "Oh shit, yeah, suck that dick. Yeah," he said as Cookie remained in the chair and masturbated her clit as he watched her. His dick seemed to swell even more in my warm mouth as I sucked it slow and hard.

"You wanna stick that big dick in this wet pussy? Huh?" Cookie asked as she inserted a finger into her wet hole. She then added, "Come fuck this pussy real quick. Let's make that dick shoot some bullets."

I cut my eyes up at him and then let him fall out of my mouth. I put a hand around it and stood up and said, "You act like you scared of all that pussy over there." I tiptoed and licked my tongue across his lips and said, "Come on, let me guide you." I kept a hold on his dick as I walked him over to Cookie. When we were in front of her, I turned my head to him and said, "Watch and learn." I then took a finger and pushed it into her while I leaned over and sucked on one of her nipples.

He said while I was stroking his nut suck, "Come on and let me get up in there."

I turned to him before pulling my finger out of her. I brushed my finger over his lips, leaving a trail of Cookie's wetness behind, and told him in a demanding voice, "Fuck that bitch good and hard."

I moved out of his way as he opened her up. The vision of his dick going in and out of her had me on edge. I got behind and dropped back down on my knees, and while listening to Cookie's cries of pleasure, I found my own. "God, yes, beat this pussy up. Push that shit deeper. Yes."

I spread his ass cheeks and licked his asshole with the point of my tongue. As I traced the wrinkled edges of it, I grabbed his nut sack and pressed on it. "Shit, you about to make me cum," he said as he pounded into her more forcefully, making it hard for me to keep my tongue in place, so I eased a finger into him instead. "What the fuck?" he asked as I caught him off guard.

Cookie then said to him in between breaths, "That finger feels good in your ass, don't it?"

He replied, "Yeah, damn it. It feels good. I'm gonna fucking cum."

I stood up and said, "Cum for me, come on and cum for me."

He pulled out of Cookie, and as he shot his cum all over her stomach, I pulled my finger out. "Holy shit. Ugh, mmm," was all he managed. I licked his cum off of her while I looked him in the eyes. "Y'all some freaky bitches. Come on, it's time to work," he said while he cleaned his dick off and then put it back in his pants.

When he walked out, I told Cookie, "Bitch, you bold as fuck."

She laughed while cleaning herself up and said, "Nah, I'm just freaky like that. Stick around and you just might learn some things."

I just shook my head and finished getting ready. We were going on stage together for the first time, and I was super hyped up about the performance. When we heard our stage names, we walked out hand in hand to the sound of Beyoncé's voice. "Let me put this ass on it. Tell ya how I feel." As Cookie and I faced each other with the pole between us, champagne was poured from above.

Cookie turned around, and as she brought her hands up over her head, I reached around and untied the front of her top. When she let go of the pole, the sheer piece of fabric fell from over her breasts. She then turned around and faced me. I squatted down, and she came and stood behind me and took off the small shirt that I was wearing. I looked up into her eyes as she pulled it from over my head. She reached her hands down and grabbed my hard nipples between her fingers and pulled on them. I reached a hand between my legs and rubbed my clit through the sheer thongs I was wearing.

Money began flying everywhere, but it didn't stop the groove we had going on. I stood back up and turned to face her with my back against the pole, and then she turned around to face the crowd of men. As she bent over and gyrated her ass into me, my clit began playing the drum again. I thought that I would go into convulsions from the pressure. I knew that I needed to cum right then. I pulled Cookie up, and when she turned around to face me, she read the look in my eyes. No words had to be spoken between us because we had made a language of our own.

She grabbed the straps of my thong and pulled them down to my ankles, and I stepped out one leg at a time. I then turned to face the pole and squatted in front of it once again. When I was all the way down, Cookie stepped to the side and let me do my thing. I stretched my legs out and sat on my ass with my thighs straddling the pole. Cookie leaned down and said to me, "Cum for me, bitch."

I bent my legs at the knees, grabbed the pole tight, and rubbed my swollen clit against the hard steel. I cried out, "Oh, yes. Mmm, shit. I'm ready to cum." Cookie came around and danced on the pole in front of me as I masturbated my clit with the pole's hardness. "I'm cumming, Cookie. Shit, I'm cumming," I hollered out to her, but I didn't know if she heard me or not. As my cum squirted out, she rubbed her hands through it then up and down the pole. I knew that we weren't supposed to take things this far when we danced, but neither of us cared.

Cookie pulled her thongs down, turned around, spread her ass cheeks, and let her ass crack clean my cum off the pole. The men were going crazy, and when I looked to the side and saw the owner, he could only shake his head. After the orgasm Cookie and I gave him earlier, there wasn't shit he could say. He could only stand there and enjoy the show along with everyone else.

When the song ended, Cookie grabbed my hand and pulled me up from the stage. My clit was still pulsing, although I had released the pressure from it. We took a moment to collect our earnings and then ran off the stage, back to our dressing room. As soon as we walked in, I said, "Girl, that was the best set ever. We should do that more often. And look at all this damn money."

Cookie smiled and responded, "Yeah, that was all that good dick we had earlier before the show." We both laughed as we cleaned up and got dressed.

We both knew that we would talk the owner into letting us do this again, and I couldn't wait. Cookie wanted to come home with me again that night, but I told her I just wanted to be alone with my thoughts. "Okay, girlfriend, I understand. But if that pussy gets to aching too much, make sure you call me, and I'll come take care of it for you," she told me as she gathered her things and walked out of the dressing room.

I finished getting myself together and then finally left the club to go home. As soon as I got there, I stripped down completely naked and got in my bed. I was exhausted from the events of the last two days and decided to catch up on some much-needed sleep. I had never came as much in my life, and it had drained me. As I lay there and thought to myself, I fell asleep with a smile on my face and wondered what I would get myself into the next time I go beyond the pole.

Chapter Three

Double the Treasure
Double the Pleasure

His dick was so far down my throat I thought I'd need the Heimlich to remove it. I had almost choked from his enormous size, but once I relaxed my throat muscles, I was good to go. He asked me sarcastically, "What's the matter? This too much dick for you?"

I ignored him and kept right on sucking like his question didn't faze me. His big dick was not going to defeat me today. I would win this battle, and I knew that if I thought about his size I would fall short of the victory. "Slurp, slurp."

Listening to the slurping sounds coming from my mouth only turned me on even more. I ran my long, manicured nails over his nut sacks as he disappeared between my lips. "Suck that dick, girl. Make that motherfucker cum." He was talking shit to me, and I loved to hear him talk it. I heard him moan and looked up to meet his gaze as he looked down upon me. "Mmm, mmm. Yes." My clit was pulsing and my pussy was dripping wet, waiting for him to put something inside of it. Then, suddenly, I felt it.

I didn't know where he came from, but when his dick slid inside of me, I flinched. However, I refused to let go of the one inside my mouth. The one who was fucking my mouth grabbed the back of me head and pushed it, and said with attitude, "Take that dick like a real bitch. Yeah, girl. Take that shit."

As I felt the man behind me slam into my body, I pushed back into him. I felt his balls slapping against my clit and bringing me closer to the eruption my pussy longed for. It wasn't long before the nigga in front of me was shooting his seeds down my throat. As I swallowed them, my pussy juice squirted out and covered the dick inside of me. When the dick slipped out of my wet pussy, it made me a little angry, but he quickly slid it into my ass, making it feel as if it had never been explored before.

That shit hurt like a muthafucker but felt good at the same time. The nigga in front of me was still talking shit, "That dick feel good to you?" He stroked his dick as he carried on, "Tell me how that dick feels so good."

"Fuck me harder. Yes." The man in front of me then slapped me in the face with his semi-hard dick, making me notice that he was well on his way to getting hard again. The one behind me suddenly pulled out, and I felt his creamy wetness cover my ass cheeks. My asshole was still throbbing from his thickness, although it was no longer there. He then rubbed his cum all over my ass with his dick. The nigga in front of me said greedily, "Man, get the fuck outta my way so I can get some of that pussy too."

I stood up and said to him, "Yeah, nigga, you can get it, but you better fuck this pussy right, or I'm gonna shame your ass." For some reason, I was gonna let him fuck me anyway. If nothing else, his size would bring me pleasure.

He let out a small laugh and said, "Yeah, you better hope that I don't shame that pussy."

He grabbed a hold of my hips while he bent me over, and as he was about to push inside of me, I interrupted his flow and asked him, "Why don't you sit down so I can show you how it's done?"

The head of his dick was already at my opening, but he pulled back a little and said, "Oh, you wanna ride this dick?" He shrugged his shoulders and then stated, "Come on then, cowgirl. Put that fat pussy on this horse." He pulled up a chair and sat down, and then leaned back with his hands intertwined behind his head.

I looked up at the dude who had just fucked me and said to him, "Don't worry. I'm not gonna leave you out of this."

I backed up my ass to the one sitting down and spread my ass cheeks. He brought a hand down and placed it around his dick, holding it straight up. His dick slowly slid right into my already wet pussy, one inch at a time. Once he was completely inside of me, I grabbed the other one's dick and pulled him closer to me. I used my leg muscles to go up and down on the dick inside of me as I sucked the one in front of me into my mouth.

"Shit, girl, you can ride real good. Yeah, ride that motherfucker," the one inside of me said, as I drooled on the one in my mouth. It took me to a whole other level, a level that hadn't been reached in a long time.

The one in my mouth began talking shit too. "Go on, girl. Shame that dick. Show that nigga what that pussy can do."

I reached my free hand down and masturbated my clit while I rode the dick to ecstasy. The one inside of me tensed up and said, "Fuck, I'm gonna cum."

I felt the pulsing and came up off of him, and then he stood up out of the chair. I turned to the side, and with both dicks in my face, I went from one to the other until both shot their cum in my face. I licked and sucked up as much of their cum as I could. "Damn, you a nasty bitch," I heard one of them say as I continued to handle business.

The taste of their cum mixed together tasted like a newly discovered fruit. They were sweet and salty and so satisfying. When they were done, I stood up from my kneeling position and walked away from them. I made sure to switch extra hard so my ass would jiggle and tease them some more. I said nothing as I walked into the bathroom and shut the door behind me.

I could faintly hear them through the door but couldn't quite understand what they had said and honestly, didn't give a fuck. They were just quick fucks to me, and if my pussy was satisfied, nothing else mattered. I loved having two men at the same time. I loved having two women too, because one partner wasn't always enough to give my body all it desired. I ran some bath water so I could relax after the good fuck I'd just had. The second man was actually a surprise to me. I didn't even know when his friend invited him over. I stepped into the bathtub and sat on the edge, and then heard the doorknob turn behind me. I acted as if I didn't hear it and proceeded doing what I was doing before the interruption. I pulled my legs apart and, as usual, my pussy opened. I reached my hand down and ran a finger up and down the length of my open slit. It was still wet and sticky from my cum, so my finger glided with ease. "Oh, yes," I moaned out loud and acted like I was still alone.

The person behind me move closer to my naked form. I didn't know which one of them it was, but soon I would welcome his presence. As I continued to slide my finger through the folds of my pussy, a hand gripped my shoulder. I cut my eyes to the side and looked at the dick. I sat there as its one eye stared into mine, looking like a snake that had slithered through the wetlands and found a nice log to perch upon. I reached my free hand up and ran a finger over the lone eye that oozed with its venom. I heard a moan escape the lips of the snake's owner, "Mmm hmmm," as I rubbed the pre-cum all over the tip. I then took my finger and sucked the pre-cum off it.

When I finally pushed my finger into my pussy, I turned my head to the side and stuck my tongue out. I ran the tip of it inside the little eye that stared at me. He took his hand and put it around his dick and lifted it up some. Then, suddenly, he dropped it back down on my shoulder again. I then heard the other one enter the bathroom. He came up behind me and placed his dick on my other shoulder. I brought my hands up and grabbed a dick with each one and started to rub the heads of them. I could feel their nut sacks laid against my back, holding on to the seeds they wanted to plant down my throat. I let their dick heads go and then got up. Their dicks tried to hold on as the skin of them stuck to mine, but I didn't want them to piggyback. I wanted them to jump all the way in and drive.

I reached down and pulled the plug out of the tub so the water could drain, and then turned on the shower. I then put my back to the wall and faced them as the water hit my body. I rolled my nipples as the water hit them with pleasure. I then looked at them seductively and said, "Y'all niggas act like you scared to come get this pussy." I took my fingers and pulled my pussy lips apart, and told them as my clit popped out, "Come on and suck this pussy real good for me." They looked at each other and then back at me before they stepped into the tub with me. The shower hit them full force as they dropped to their knees. I stood and waited to see just how it would play out. Suddenly, I felt both of their tongues on my clit at the same time. It felt so good and like nothing I'd ever had. I cried out in pleasure, "Oh god, yes. Oh, it feels so good. Yes, yes, mmm." I was weakened by their gesture and had to let my pussy lips go because I couldn't hold on any longer.

I placed a hand on each one of their heads and let them do their thing. I felt a finger go into my pussy and then one went into my asshole. I cried out even louder, "I can't take it, shit. This feels so good. Fuck me good, yes." My legs felt weak and I didn't think that I could stand any longer. I knew that I was about to cum, and I also knew that when I did, it would steal all of my strength. "Fuck, I'm about to cum, yesss," I yelled one last time before my cum squirted out of me. They tried to catch it with their tongues, but the shower water quickly rinsed it away and down the drain. I barely had time to catch my breath before I was bent over the side of the tub.

The other one stepped out and stood in front of me, his stiff dick was in his hand, waiting for me to take over. The other man stood behind me, talking shit. "I'm about to fuck this pussy real good." He then pushed his length into me really hard. So hard that my head slammed into the man in front of me.

"Oh god, yes, Beat this pussy up. Fuck it good for me, please. Yes."

The one in front of me, good and ready, said, "Girl, come on and suck this dick, quit playing." I cut my eyes up at him before pulling him into my mouth and sucking extra hard.

The dick behind me pulled out and shot cum all in my ass crack, as he said, "Shit, I didn't want to nut that quick, but this pussy ain't give me no choice." He then slapped me on my ass and told the one in front of me, "Come on, dawg, let's switch spots so you can get your shit off."

The one in my mouth pulled out and switched with him, and then said to me, "My partner got that pussy, but I'm an ass man, so I'm about to give that ass a beating." He rubbed the head of his dick up and down my ass crack and then finally pushed it into my asshole.

"Ugh, shit," I cried out as he opened my ass wide. The one now in front of me was semi-hard because he'd already gotten his, so I sucked on his balls, trying to help him get back right.

The nigga behind me was pounding into me hard and talked to me at the same time. "You like this big dick up in that ass?" He thrust a couple more times and asked again, "You gon' answer me, huh? You like this dick up in that ass?"

I let the man's balls fall out of my mouth because it was hard to keep my grip on them. The man behind me pounded into me so hard I could barely answer him, but I knew that I must. "Yes, oh god, yes. I love it. I fucking love this shit! Fuck me, motherfucker. Fuck me."

He finally began to slow a little and said, in between breaths, "I'm, shit, I'm, I'm about to cum all in this ass. Damn, girl." His nails gripped the skin on my ass so hard I just knew that he would leave scars.

"Man, fuck this shit," the one in front of me stated right before he walked out of the bathroom, mad because he couldn't get his dick back hard.

"Ugh, yes, yes," I cried out as the man inside of me began to cum all in my asshole, making it wet and slippery. I had been turned the shower water off, but when he pulled his dick out of me, I reached over and turned it back on.

"Damn, girl, that shit was good. You make a nigga wanna stick around."

I looked at him like he was crazy and said, "Nah, nigga, ain't gonna be no sticking around here. I like to keep my options open." I paused long enough to flash a smile at him, and then said, "The dick was good though." And then we shared a laugh.

As the hot water hit our bodies, we washed off our indiscretions and then got out and dried off before getting dressed. When we left the bathroom and went back to the main room, his friend was putting his shoes on and looked embarrassed about his performance. I kinda felt bad for him, so I tried to make him feel better by saying, "It's all good, champ. That dick was on point no matter what."

He shook his head and replied, "Next time, I'm gonna fuck the shit out of you. You can believe that." We all shared a laugh before the two of them left me to my thoughts. I decided to lay down for a little while before going to my friend's place and checking on her. We usually fucked niggas together, but today I wanted the dick to myself. I needed to be fucked hard, and they surely delivered.

I woke up a few hours later to my cell phone ringing. "Hello," I answered in a groggy voice.

"Bitch, when you coming over? I got a fine ass bitch over here from out of town, and she is freaky as fuck," my friend said.

"Now you know my pussy is already wet. Girl, I am on my way." I hung up and went to take a quick shower, and then got out and brushed my teeth. While putting my toothbrush back in its holder, my clit begin to throb. I knew that I should wait, but the ridges lining the holder were calling name.

I lifted my leg up onto the toilet seat and when I spread my pussy lips, I began to rub the ridges of the holder against my swollen clit. "Shit. Yes. Ssss." I never thought a tooth-brush holder could make me cum, but the roughness of it on my tender, raw flesh had me going. "Mmm hmmm. Mmm." As I continued to rub it over my clit, I stuck a finger into my pussy. It only took a few seconds for my cum to cover the finger I had inside of me. I was far from average when it came to sex, so the orgasm gave me a fresh boost of energy. I didn't even take the time to wash the cum off me. I just pulled my panties up and let them soak up all the moisture.

My clit kept throbbing from the orgasm I had just given it. I had to push my sexual energy to the side until I made it to my destination, where I knew I would curb my sexual appe-tite. It felt like the ride to her place took forever. I was still so horny that I thought about stopping a couple of times and handling my business, but instead, I continued to push the gas. Once I finally pulled up to her building, I jumped out and walked to her door at a fast pace. My clit throbbed harder with each step.

"Who is it?" I heard her ask over the music that played in the background.

"Bitch, it's me. Open the door," I yelled loudly, so she could hear me.

When she pulled the door open, she said, "Girl, get your ass in here. You about to have a good time." She smiled as her sheer robe opened a little and a nipple peeked out at me. I walked out and bent over a little and brushed my tongue across the exposed flesh. "Ole freaky, anxious ass," my friend said as she closed the door behind me.

I then stripped my clothes off and asked, "Girl, where is the fun happening at? This pussy is already wet and ready." She dropped her robe and grabbed my hand, pulling me to the guest room.

There on the bed was one of the prettiest and thickest redbones I had ever seen. She laid there with her legs already spread and pussy wet and waiting. When we walked in, the redbone said, "Damn, girl, this pussy is tired of waiting. Are you gonna come finish what you started?"

My friend walked over to the bed and got on it, but before she went down between the girl's legs, she turned to me and said, "Sorry. I was in the middle of lunch when you knocked." She pushed a finger into the redbone and then turned back to me and said, "Care to join me?"

I shrugged my shoulders and went to the bed where they were at. The redbone was twisting her nipples with her eyes looking at me, and asked, "You wanna cum too? Come on and let me suck that pussy real good and make it squirt."

I didn't hesitate at all. Instead, I got up on the bed and straddled her face, and when I grabbed the headboard, she took her hands and spread my pussy lips. My clit popped out and went right into her mouth. I could feel her flicking her tongue over it real fast. "Oh, shit. Yeah, that feels so good," I said to her as I rotated my hips over her face.

I heard my friend say from behind me, "That shit feels good, don't it?"

I cried out, "Yes, it does feel good."

The redbone began to suck my clit hard, and she must have been cumming because she was moaning really loud, "Mmm, mmm, hmmm."

Not even a minute later, I could feel my head getting dizzy, and I knew I was about to cum. "Oh my god, I'm gonna cum. Yes, yes, I'm cumming," I yelled out as my cum coated the red bone's chin. She refused to let go of my clit, and I felt as if I would faint. It was one of the most intense orgasms I'd ever had. I finally was able to pull up from her. "Damn, bitch. You ain't wanna let my shit go. What the fuck?" I said to her once I escaped the hold her mouth had on me.

She said in response, "Shit shouldn't have been so good to my taste buds."

We all shared a laugh, and then my friend got on her knees beside the redbone and took one of the girl's massive breasts in her hand. She pulled it to her as she opened her pussy up. She then put the redbone's fat nipple up to her clit and rubbed it across. I had never seen a female masturbate with a nipple before, but she definitely enjoyed herself. I got behind her and slid my arms under hers and around her. I said in her ear, "It's a shame we got all this pussy in here and no dick to put in it."

She said back to me, "I can fix that."

She stopped what she was doing and got up from the bed. She then grabbed her cell phone and put a number in it, and said to the person on the other end. "What's up, nigga? There's some wet ass pussy over here that needs something long and thick deep inside of it. You feel like cumming?" I didn't know what he said in return, but what man in his right mind would turn down some pussy? She looked from me to the redbone and smiled, while saying, "There's a nice long dick on the way, girls." We all shared a laugh, anticipating his arrival.

Not even twenty minutes later, we heard a knock at the door. All three of us walked to answer it because we were ready to fuck the dick that was outside of it. When my friend opened it, there stood a dark-chocolate masterpiece. His shirt was unbuttoned, revealing his chiseled flesh. I looked down to his crotch and saw a bulge, making my pussy jump. As we all stood there and looked at him, I finally broke the trance and said, while pushing past the door, "I want to sit on that motherfucker." I grabbed one of his hands and pulled him through the door. I shut the door behind us and pulled his shirt off. I said, "Y'all acting like you don't know what to do, so just stand your asses right there and watch a real bitch at work." I reached around his waistline and undid his jeans, and then asked him, "Do you mind?"

"Hell nah," he replied as he held his hands up in surrender.

My friend and the redbone came closer as I said, "Damn, bitch. You called all this dick over here and now you act like you don't know what to do with it."

She replied, "Nah, this ain't the nigga I summoned."

He finally spoke up and said, "Ya boy was busy, so he sent me."

She ran her hand down his chest and told him, "Well, I damn sure ain't mad about it."

She and the redbone grabbed a hold of his pants and pulled them down to his ankles. He stepped out of them, and

I threw them to the side. The girls started to suck his nipples as I came back up and spread his ass cheeks just enough to run my tongue up the crack of it. "Shit," I heard him say as I came all the way up.

I reached back around him and put my hand around his dick. It was so thick and so hard, and I couldn't wait to have it inside of me. The women both dropped to their knees and asked, "What you want us to do with this dick, daddy?"

"Let me show you what to do with it," he said as he put a hand on each of their heads. He then told them, "I want y'all to suck this muthafucker, shit. What you mean?"

I slowly stroked his massive member and lifted it up as the other two women pulled his nuts into their mouths. I took my free hand and ran it back down his ass crack a couple of times, stopping at his hole but not going in, at least not yet. I'd save that treat for later. I went around to the front of him while he moaned from the pleasure of the two enforcers invading his nut sack. "Mmm, yeah. That shit feels so damn good."

He slowly grinded his hips as I leaned over the other two women and licked the pre-cum off his dick, and then asked him, "Are you gonna cum for me if I suck it really good for you?"

He looked down at me as I cut my eyes up at him. He replied, "I don't know. It depends on how good you gonna suck it."

I licked the head again as my hand went up and down his length, and said hungrily, "Nigga, I'm gonna suck the skin off this bitch."

I then pulled the head of his dick into my mouth and sucked as hard as I could. My friend and the redbone came up and licked the length of him as I moved my hand out of the way for them. "Yeah, suck that dick for me. That shit feels good," he said as the two quit licking him and went back to his nut sack as his dick found my tonsils. "Damn, you about to make me cum all down your throat. Suck that dick, baby, damn," he cried out as I continued to lick and suck his manhood. I felt his dick pulse and was ready to drink his juice. My stomach was growling and needed something inside of it. "Shit, I'm cumming. Go ahead and catch that shit," he said to me as I swallowed some of it down my throat.

"Mmm, mmm," I moaned with each gulp. I then let his dick go so the other two women could come up and get them a taste. They sucked him until he was drained.

"Damn," was all he said as we all got up and walked away from him. We all walked back to the bedroom as he followed with his dick in his hand, trying to stroke it back to life.

I told him, "You ain't gotta do all that. This pussy 'bout to give you some CPR and bring you back."

I was selfish and wanted him to fuck me first, so I told my friend to lay on the bed and spread her legs. The redbone got up and straddled her face as I bent over in between my friend's legs. As we all savored each other's essence, he got behind me and spread my ass cheeks, causing my pussy lips to open with it. I moaned in pleasure as he bent down behind me and stuck his tongue into my pussy hole, "Mmm, hmmm."

He came up long enough to say, "I'm gonna tear all this pussy up."

Once he was hard again, he stood up and rubbed his dick in between my ass cheeks. My pussy was wet as fuck as it waited to be opened wide by the beast he possessed. The other two women on the bed in front of me were a distant memory as his dick entered me. I took my mouth off the pussy in front of me and gripped the sheets as he filled my walls. "Oh, god, oh, oh, yes. Fuck this pussy. Yes," I called out as my friend and the red bone got up off the bed. I knew they wanted a piece of the dick too, but I wasn't thinking about them.

They got behind him as he pounded into me and dropped to their knees again. They played with his balls and licked his asshole as he fucked me good and hard. "This dick feel good to you? Huh? You like this dick?" he asked as my pussy sucked him in.

I cried out, "Oh god, yes. This dick good as fuck. Make this pussy cum on that dick." He slammed into me harder as I reached my peak and yelled, "I'm cumming. Oh, fuck. This pussy's cumming. Ugh, yes." I gripped the sheets tighter as my cum squirted out all over his dick.

He slowed down as I trembled in front of him, and then he finally pulled out, still hard and covered in my juice. I moved from in front of him and lay down. My friend got up and said, "'Bout damn time, bitch. Being greedy with the dick and shit. We all want a little bit of that." She then lay down on the bed in front of him and propped her head up on my thigh. She pulled her legs up to her chest and told him, "Nigga, you ain't done. Think that dick can handle two more pussies?"

He rubbed a finger over her clit and said, "Shit, this dick can handle a whole harem. Go ahead and open that pussy up."

She reached in between her bent legs and spread her pussy lips as the red bone put her hand around his dick and said, "Don't give it all to her. I want some too."

She held onto him as he slid inside the pussy in front of him. I played with my nipples as I watched his dick pound into my friend. "Damn. This dick is good. Fuck me. Yes, fuck me." The redbone reached down and rubbed on my friend's clit as she took the dick. It didn't take her but a second to cum all over his dick, and when he pulled out, the red bone leaned down and licked the cum off. My friend gained her composure and got up off the bed and said, "Girl, you right, I ain't never came that quick."

The nigga licked his sexy ass lips and asked the red bone, "What's the matter, Red? You hesitating like you scared of this dick."

She raised her eyebrows and looked up at him crazy, and said as she climbed on the bed, "Nah, nigga. I want that dick up this ass. Can you handle this ass?"

She bent over and spread her ass cheeks wide, as he told her, "Nah, can that ass handle this dick?"

He rubbed on her pussy first and then slid a finger into her hole as her wetness covered it. "Mmm, yeah. That feels good," she cried out as I lay there and watched him perform again. This nigga had me mesmerized by his gangsta. I planned on inviting him to my place afterward, because I wanted to sit on that dick all night.

He caught me staring and asked, "What's the matter, you need some more of this?"

I smiled and told him, "Do what you do. I wanna take it home and sleep with it up in this pussy."

He put the head of his dick to Red's asshole, and before he pushed into her, he said to me, "It's all good. I could use a night cap. That pussy can be my pajamas."

I heard Red cry out from the force of him entering her. "Ugh, shit." He pulled in and out her ass slowly while keeping his eyes locked onto mine. I usually liked having two men at the same time, but his fuck game and his big dick would make up for the absence.

Their bodies slapped together and broke my trance. Red continued to cry out in either pleasure or pain, "Fuck. Damn, this dick is good, ugh yes. I'm gonna cum." He fucked her so good that she pulled her own hair.

I came up off the bed and got on my knees beside Red and told him, "Cum for me. Go ahead. Make that dick cum for me."

He went faster when Red started squirting her cum out, and then he finally pulled out and came all over her ass cheeks. "Huh, shit," he said while he breathed heavily.

My friend had left the room after he piped her down, but now she came back. She walked over to the bed and licked some of his cum off of Red's ass. I reached over and ran a finger through the wetness before bringing it back to my lips, and then I sucked the cum off. I asked him, "Did you have a good time, daddy?"

He twisted one of my nipples between his fingers and said, "Yeah. But I feel like I'm gonna have an even better one later." I smiled because I knew just what he meant.

We all finally went and got cleaned up and were leaving one at a time. I gave the nigga my number and address before he walked out. I turned to my friend and said, "Thanks, I had a good time, but what happened to the nigga that was supposed to show?"

She rolled her eyes at the thought and said, "Bitch, that nigga passed up on some pussy to go see a basketball game, so he sent his homie instead."

I just shook my head and said to her, "Well, the replacement was damn good." We shared a laugh together and then hugged. I left to go prepare myself for the good dick I would enjoy later.

I was on the road again, but this time headed back to where I came from. My pussy throbbed to the beat of the music that came from my speakers. The rendezvous I had earlier with my friend and the red bone was something I'd always remember, but the dick I would be riding later on tonight, that was all I could think about as my pussy got wet. I couldn't wait for another second or even go one more mile without another orgasm.

I pulled into the parking lot of a convenience store and got out. I went in and asked to use their restroom. Their cashier pointed me in the direction I needed to go. When I went in, I noticed that there were two stalls instead of just a single toilet. The nervousness of another coming in to use the facilities made my adrenaline spike. "Oh well, fuck it," I said to myself as I entered a stall and shut the door. I then secured the lock and pulled my pants down, removing one leg so I could prop it up. I put a foot on the toilet seat after I put my shoe back on and went to work. "Ugh, yes, sss." As I sped up, I heard the door open, but I just couldn't stop. It felt too good to end it, and I was close to cumming. "Mmm, hmmm." I tried not to moan too loud, but I just couldn't help myself. A sudden knock at the stall door broke me from the spell my finger had on my clit. I was pissed because I wanted to cum so bad.

I removed my shoe and pulled my pants leg back on and then put my shoe back on. I then opened the door with an attitude, and asked as I did, "Can a bitch play with they own pussy without being disturbed? Damn."

I looked up and froze from surprise as the intruder stated, "Damn, a nigga just trying to help you out. I couldn't wait till later, so I followed you." I couldn't form any words as I stared into the eyes of the nigga from earlier. I just grabbed a fistful of his shirt, pulled him in, and shut the stall door behind us so our night could begin.

Sugar E. Walls

Chapter Four

Lustful Loyalty

My nipples were hard, my pussy was wet. My man was beside me, asleep. From under the sheet that was thrown over him, his dick was looking at me and daring me to violate it. I didn't want to wake him but damn, I needed to cum.

My nails were long from a fresh manicure. I took one and circled the head of his dick with it, but that wasn't enough for me to be pleased. I was greedy and wanted what I wanted whenever the fuck I wanted it. I spread my legs, and my pussy lips slightly opened. My clit head was plump and poking out, and I licked the tip of my finger before pulling back the hood on it, exposing the raw meat underneath. I lay my finger upon it and said in a low tone, "Oh, yes," still trying not to wake him. I then pressed down and made slow, circular motions, massaging the aching feeling. "Shit," I said as my breathing became heavier.

I closed my eyes and imagined his lips upon me, sucking on my pussy, and then I felt it. A pressure that I was not giving. I didn't want to open my eyes because I was afraid that the sensation would disappear. "Oh, yes. Fuck me," I said to myself, louder than I had meant to. This felt too good to be my imagination, so I finally opened my eyes just enough to peek and make sure it was really happening, and there he was. His finger long and fat inside my essence as it made macaroni sounds from my wetness. I smiled at him and said, "I thought you'd never wake up."

He smiled his sexy smile at me and said, "Go ahead, baby, let me watch you play with that pussy." He then pulled his finger out of me and put it in his mouth, sucking off the moisture my pussy had left behind.

I said to him in a seductive voice, "Okay, boo, I'm about to give you the show of your life." I reached over to the nightstand and pulled open the drawer. I removed a silver dildo from inside and laughed as his eyes stretched wider. I asked him, "Can you fuck me like this silver rocket's about to?"

He leaned back on his elbows and said, "Fuck that pussy, and then I'm gonna show you how it's really done." He smiled that sexy, seductive smile that always made my insides melt, and for a second, I was stuck just staring at him.

I secured the round metal in my small hand and rubbed it on my clit. The coldness sent chill bumps up my spine and made the hairs on my arms stand up. "Ugh, ooh, yeah," I said, as I closed my eyes into small slits, leaving them open just enough to peek at him. My pussy was so wet I could feel my juices draining down a little further so I could rub into the wetness. It now shined as if it had been freshly coated with wax and buffed to shine brighter.

"Damn, baby, that pussy is so wet, just the way I like it," he said as I brought the rocket back up to my clit and pressed it against the throbbing flesh.

I said seductively, while I opened my eyes all the way and stared deep into his, "Yeah, you wanna fuck this wet pussy, don't you?"

As I moved the toy closer to my hole, he said, "Go ahead, baby. Show your nigga what that wet ass pussy can do."

I smiled and stated, "I thought you'd never ask." I then inserted the tip of the rocket into my pussy and pushed it little by little inside. "Oh, yes. Sss, mmm, yes," I moaned from the cold hardness entering me.

"Yeah, baby, fuck yeah," I heard him in the background as I pulled the rocket in and out slowly, coating it with more of my juice. I reached down with my other hand and stroked my clit as I fucked my pussy harder. "Oh god, yes, yes. I'm gonna cum, baby. I'm gonna cum," I screamed out but never stopped my rhythm.

I saw him sit all the way up as he said, "Cum for me. Go ahead, baby, cum for me." He grabbed a hold of my knees, one hand on each, and spread my legs as far as he could. The air conditioner was on and the ceiling fan was spinning, but I felt like I was in a furnace from the heat of my body. As my cum squirted out onto the silver beast, I called out to him, "I'm cumming. Oh, baby, it feels so good. Yes, yes. I'm cumming."

The spot beneath me was soaked from the juices that flowed from me. Suddenly, I felt him grab my wrist and pull. As the rocket left my inner darkness, I heard him say, "Save some of that cum for this dick."

I let out a small laugh and said back to him, "There's always enough cum in this pussy for you." I took the rocket and rubbed it across his mouth before I put it in mine. He came closer to me as he licked my essence from his lips. His tongue, fat and pink, reminding me of the skills it possessed and wanting it to touch my woman hood.

I hungrily asked him, "Baby, are you gonna put that tongue game down on this pussy or what?"

He looked at me as he stroked his long dick and said, "Oh yeah. Now you know I'm gonna taste that pussy before I fill it up." He bent down, and as he did, I spread my pussy lips open wide. My clit popped out like the head of a turtle and awaited his touch.

As soon as he sucked my pearl into his mouth, I almost lost my breath. My heart sped up as if it were racing against the orgasm I knew was soon to come. "Yes, baby, oh god, yes, make this pussy cum again."

I listened to the sounds of his mouth sucking me into another zone. When a finger entered me, I lifted my ass up a little off the bed and met his motion. I rotated my hips as the pressure began to build again, and it only took a few seconds for my pussy to open the flood gates. "I'm cumming, suck it, baby, don't stop. I'm cumming," I hollered out as he continued to suck while my cum squirted out on his finger. I was used to getting multiple orgasms every time he touched me. No other man had ever made me experience that before. He kept sucking my clit until my heartbeat slowed and my waterfall ceased. He then ran his tongue down the length of my slit and removed his finger as he licked up the cream he had whipped up.

He finally came up for air and I propped myself up and told him, "Let me suck that volcano before I make it erupt in this pussy." I loved to suck his dick because it fit so perfectly in my mouth. My deep throat was on point when it came to him, and I couldn't wait for it to touch the back of my throat. I got up and bent over with my ass pointing up in the air.

Before I could get his dick between my lips, he bent and grabbed my ass cheeks and spread them. He let one go only long enough to run a finger down my ass crack and into my asshole as he asked me, "Can Daddy get a little of that too?"

I told him, as he pulled his finger out and then came back up to where his dick was directly in front of my face, "You can get anything you want from me."

I then pulled his dick into my mouth and as I sucked him, I ran my tongue over the lining of the head, tracing its edges. I cupped his balls and pulled on them like I was milking a cow, and in a way, I kinda was. "Yeah, baby, suck that dick. That shit feels so damn good. This your dick. Suck your dick. Yes," he said as he slammed his pelvis into my face. I sucked him hard and fast and when I felt the pulsing of his vein, I sucked even harder. "I'm about to cum. Don't stop, swallow it for me. Fuck. I'm cumming, baby." As his seeds shot out, I let them slide down my throat with ease. His cum always quenched my undying thirst. The sweat on my forehead dripped down into my eyes and tried to steal my view, but there was nothing that could blind me from his masculine form. I slowed down as the last of his liquid left the inside of him. He reached a hand up and into my hair, stroking it and saying, "Damn, baby. That shit was on point."

I finally let him fall out of my mouth and laid back on the bed, the softness of the pillows behind me. He came and lay beside me and said, "You always know how to make a nigga feel good." I turned on my side and wrapped his semi-hard dick in my hand. I wasn't through, and I knew that he wasn't either. "That's right. Good ahead and get it ready for that pussy," he said as he reached over and pinched one of my nipples hard.

It hurt so good when he did that to me. He rolled it between his manly fingers as I stuck my tongue out and licked one of his. My clit began to throb as he continued to play with my nipples, taking a few seconds with each one. I stroked his dick hard but slow, trying to bring him back to life, as I said, "I want this dick inside of me forever."

He let go of my nipples and said, "Come sit on my chest so I can lick that ass one good time." I always did as he asked because they say, what you won't do the next one will, and I'd be damned if I made room for another bitch to pleasure my man. Whatever it took to make him happy and to feel good, was exactly what I did. My loyalty to him could never be questioned in any situation. I got up from beside him and straddled his chest backward, my ass positioned right at his face. I continued to stroke his dick with one hand and his balls with the other as I felt the tip of his tongue glide down my ass crack. He licked from the top to the bottom and then around the wrinkles of my asshole. The wetness of his tongue and the coolness of the breeze from the ceiling fan made my insides flutter. He inhaled my scent and said before gliding a finger inside of me, "Suck it for me, baby. Get it back right so I can fuck you real good."

I didn't say anything because I couldn't. I was so gone into his world that no words could be formed. I only moaned as I sucked him once again into my mouth, "Mmm hmm, mmm," I moaned loudly in pleasure as his finger touched the hidden places inside of me.

"That's it, baby. Do your thang. That's your dick and can't 'nere 'notha bitch fuck with it," he said, egging me on as I felt him growing and stiffening under my touch. "I'm gonna fuck that pussy so good for you," he stated as he pulled his finger out of me and then spanked me on the ass. I let his dick fall out of my mouth and came up. I moved my body down so my pussy would be closer to his ever-growing manhood. I kept my back turned to him so he could watch his dick in action once it found its way inside of me.

I planted one foot on either side of him and spread my legs. I grabbed his dick in my hand and opened my pussy lips. "Uh, yes," I moaned as I beat on my swollen clit with the head of his dick. He gripped my back tightly with his fingers and squeezed. I leaned my head back and took my other hand and gripped his balls, pulling them up as if I were trying to rip them off a tree branch. They were so thick and so full of my favorite drink.

As I pressed and pulled, I heard him say from behind me, "Come on, baby. Plant me in that beautiful garden." I let his balls go and placed a hand on his thigh for balance as I lifted up enough to put the head of his dick to my entrance. I then put my other hand on his other thigh and watched as he disappeared inside of me.

"Mmm, baby," I moaned as his thick black dick opened me and began to explore its territory. Every single time with him felt like my first time with him.

"Yes, baby, yes," he cried out as he came off the bed with his hips meeting me thrust for thrust. "That dick feel good to you?" he asked me with a little authority in his voice.

I answered, "Yes, oh god, yes."

He wasn't satisfied with my answer, so he said more aggressively, "Nah. Get up and put that ass up so I can make your ass tell me how it really feels." When I came up off of him, he slapped me on the ass again and then got up off the bed. He stood up on the side, his dick still sticking straight out ready to do some damage. I got on all fours and turned my ass to him so he could do to me what he did best, fuck me real good.

He didn't ease himself into me but instead, once the head of his dick was at my wet dripping hole, he rammed it in. I almost lost my breath from the force of his massive member. I grabbed my nipples and pulled on them as I told him, "Fuck this pussy hard, muthafucker. Make this pussy cum."

His balls slammed into my clit as his inner beast came out. "This dick feel good to you? Huh? You want this dick to fuck you harder?" he asked in between thrusts.

"Yes, please. Oh god. Please fuck this pussy harder. I love it when this dick fucks me rough," I cried out to him louder. I could feel the stinging sensation from the force of his body ramming into mine, causing a numbing effect. I took a hand from my nipple and went down and pinched my clit so hard I thought I would bust it open. His dick was hurting so good inside of me as he continued his battle with my pussy walls.

"Oh yes. Yes. Fuck me. Mmm, yes," I continued to holler out as all of his goodness had me on edge.

He then asked, "You want me to cum in this good ass pussy?"

He reached up and grabbed a handful of my hair as I told him what he wanted to hear, "Yes, daddy, please fill this pussy up with your cum. Cum all in this pussy, mmm hmm."

No sooner than I said it, he yanked my head back and went still. He then pulled back a little and slammed back into me hard as he squeezed his ass muscles and shot his creamy essence inside of me. "Oh, fuck, I'm cumming. Shit," he yelled out as I felt his pulsing dick coat my walls with its liquid and water my garden. When all was drained from him, he let go of my hair and let his dick fall out of me, leaving my hole open and dripping with his nectar.

I lay flat on my stomach so I could catch my breath, and he came up on the bed to lay beside me. I looked at him and said, "I love it when you fuck me hard like that."

I smiled as he responded, "That pussy's so damn good I can't help it." We stayed there for a few minutes and ended up falling asleep into the deep slumber we so desperately needed. I knew we would have another session when we woke, it always happened that way.

It felt like only a few minutes had passed when something wet touched my exposed nipple. I opened my eyes into small slits and caught his eyes looking back at me. "Come on, baby, let's go take a shower together," he said as he sucked my nipple between his lips.

I smiled at him and started to get up, but he blocked my way. I said to him, "I thought you was ready to go get cleaned up." He shrugged his shoulders and then moved his hands, holding them up as if I was an officer of the law apprehending him. I kissed the tip of his nose and then sucked his bottom lip into my mouth. Every part of him tasted sweet to me no matter the time of day or night. I had never tasted anything sweeter. I got off the bed as he sat there looking disappointed, like I had just given him his first broken heart. I asked him, "What's the matter, baby? You look like you need a little something to make you smile."

I propped one leg up on the edge of bed and pulled one of my pussy lips to the side. As if on cue, my clit popped out and exposed itself to its master. "That's what the fuck I'm talking about," he said in that sexy, masculine voice of his. I could tell that his mouth was watering, wanting to taste my early morning juices. The nectar inside sweet from marinating all night in its hive.

I looked at him in a sly manner and said, "You wanna taste this honey, don't you?" He only nodded his head and then came closer to the edge of the bed where my foot was positioned. I moved my leg a bit so he could sit comfortably where he landed and then put my leg back up. My foot rested between his legs. His dick laid across it as if it was a blanket keeping me warm.

I motioned a finger for him to come a little closer and told him seductively, "Come put your nose to it and smell it, baby." He leaned over until his face was right up on it and rubbed his nose over my clit and inhaled the sexual aroma as his dick swelled larger on my foot. I took the palm of my hand and pushed his head back, telling him, "Nah, daddy, you ain't touching this pussy right now. I'm gonna make it cum without you."

He looked up at me innocently and said, "Come on, baby, don't do that. What's up with that shit?" I didn't answer him but instead, I pulled the hood back on my clit and spit on a finger of my other hand. I put so much on it that a spit line formed, and as I pulled my finger away, it drew the line with it like a string and then dropped on my chest. He reached up and ran a fingertip over the wasted saliva and then rubbed it into one of my nipples. I knew it was hard for him to contain himself, but I didn't want him to make me cum just yet.

I put my spit-covered finger over the exposed meat of my clit and rubbed it back and forth. "Ooh, yes," I said as the pleasure took me out of this world. I forgot about the man in front of me for a moment as I pressed down hard and made myself cum quickly. "Sss. Yes." I felt his hand rub my dripping cum into my inner thigh, coating it like it was moisturizer. I was then brought back to the real world and looked down at him. I smiled a half smile and dropped my leg down from the edge of the bed. I turned around and walked away from him because I knew he would soon follow.

I heard him ask, "What the fuck you doing?" as I disappeared from his view. I went into the bathroom, and as I bent over the tub to get it ready, I felt him. He grabbed a hold of my hips and opened me up with his hardness and said, "You thought I was gonna let all this pussy walk away from me and not follow it?" He thrust into me with a vengeance and said, "Nah, lil' mama. I'ma fuck this pussy one way or the other."

My breasts moved up and down as he moved behind me. "Yes. I love it when you take this pussy. Beat this pussy up, baby. Make it squirt for you," I told him hungrily while I tried to keep my balance at the same time. I had my hands placed on the edge of the tub as he made it hard for me to keep my grip.

His dick tore my pussy walls down as he talked shit behind me. "This is my pussy and I fuck it when I want like I want, and ain't shit you can do about it." My ass rode in waves from the vibration as he continued on with his tirade. "Tell me who the fuck this pussy belongs to. Tell me, damnit."

I tried to play hard because I loved it when he punished me with his hardness, but finally, I told him, "This is your pussy, baby, and you fuck it so good. Make your pussy cum. Yes, baby, fuck it and make it cum." He slammed into me one last time, and I almost lost my grip. I breathed heavy as he filled me with his love juice. He stayed inside of me for a few minutes, his hands holding onto my hips, and refused to let go. I had known that I would pay for walking away from him, and punishment was well worth it.

We finally turned the shower on and enjoyed the essence of the water. As it hit our bodies, my pussy still throbbed from his undulation, and I knew that his performance would leave me sore. I didn't mind being sore from his good dick because there was no pain that brought me a greater pleasure. I washed his body and then paid close attention to his dick and balls. The soap suds covering them like a sweater on a cold day. I kissed him and said, "You fucked me so good, baby. I feel like I owe you one."

I laughed as he said to me, "Then maybe you should pay up." I quickly dropped to my knees, and as the water attacked my body, my mouth attacked his dick. I sucked him so hard he lost his balance and had to sit down on the edge of the tub. His balls hung like ripe apples waiting to be picked and eaten, as he pressed my head down into him, and when he began to pulse, I came up and sucked only the head as I used my hand to jack the length of him. Suddenly, his warm cum shot out and traveled down my throat. I sucked him until nothing else came out. When he was done, I released him from my mouth and looked up into his eyes just in time for him to smile at me and say lovingly, "Debt paid."

Sugar E. Walls

Chapter Five

Mojado Española Cono
(Wet Spanish Pussy)

I had been sitting on my leather sofa watching the playoff game I had been waiting for, when I heard a sudden knock at my door. "Who is it?" I yelled out, but I never took my eyes off the big screen that was in front of me. I tried to ignore the knock, but it suddenly came again. "Shit, this better be good," I said to myself as I jumped up and went to answer the door. I yanked that motherfucker open with great force while I asked, "Damn. Who the fuck is it?"

Her eyes widened in fear as she stood before me looking flawless and beautiful. Her deep black hair hung to her ass with the small curly ringlets brushing against it, lightly even in her still stance. I had no clue who this chick was, but I was mesmerized by her presence. I finally formed enough words to ask, "Yo, shawty, what's up? Can I help you with something?"

She answered me in an innocent yet seductive voice, "Lo siento." (I'm sorry.)

Her Spanish accent was deep, and I could feel my dick slowly begin to rise. I had no clue what she had just said to me, but I responded the best way I could. "Um, I have no clue what the fuck you just said." I paused and then asked her, "Can you say it in English?"

She walked in and came close to me and placed her hand over my dick, and then said, as I stood there wide eyed and stuck, "Anoche te vi en el cine apapachando a tu novia." (I saw everything with your girlfriend at the movies last night). My dick got hard instantly as I tried to pull back from her. She

77

grabbed the side of the door, slammed it closed, and then said, "No se' por que' hoy estoy tan cachando." (I don't know why I feel so horny today).

She proceeded to come closer to me as I stood there in shock and said, "Um, I think maybe you have the wrong apartment."

She placed her hand back on my dick and said, "Ah, tu es muy duro." (You are very hard). As she unzipped my zipper, my mouth watered. "Mejor cierra la puerta con llaue, por si acaso," (Better lock the door just in case,) she said as she turned around and walked back to my door. I thought that maybe she was going to leave and became disappointed, but she only locked the door instead.

When she turned back to me, she took off the dress she was wearing and stood there in front of me completely naked. "What the fuck is happening here?" I said in a low voice, mainly to myself since she couldn't understand me. Her body was gorgeous and she was thick where it counted. Her dark areolas that circled her plump nipples gave her body a pleasant glow. Her pussy hair was healthily trimmed on her plump pussy lips. She reached a hand down between her legs and spread her pussy open and said, "Sivase todo lo que quiera, por favor." (Help yourself to anything you want).

She walked back up to me and was so close I could smell the mint on her breath, as if she had just brushed her teeth. She brought her hands to the button and zipper on my pants and undid them all the way before she pushed them down around my ankles. I stepped out of them one leg at a time because I didn't know what else to do. I'd never had a strange woman show up at my door before and do the type of shit she was doing. All I knew was that I couldn't resist her even if I would have tried.

With my pants off and my dick sticking straight out, I just stood there wondering what her next move would be. She turned and walked away from me again, but this time she went to my couch and sat down on the back of it. "Yo, this is really strange, and I'm not exactly sure what you want me to do. I mean, I think I know, but I'm not sure," I rambled on nervously as I watched her lift a leg up and prop it on the back of couch where she was sitting.

Her clit, nice and fat, popped out and stared at me, as she said, "Esto es lo que ofrezco. To'melo o dejelo." (This is what I have to offer, take it or leave it.) I could see her pussy juice glistening in the dim light as she put a finger in her mouth, licked it, and then put it on her clit and massaged. "Oh si, si," (Oh yes, yes,) she said as she looked me deep in the eyes.

I decided to just go with the flow and walked over to her. I gently slid a finger into her open wet hole as she continued to talk to me in a language I didn't understand. "Tu amiga es muy tacana. Lleuo mucho tiempo esperando." (Your girlfriend is extremely stingy. I've waited a long time.) I slid my finger in and out a little faster as her pussy juice coated it. She put a hand behind my head and pulled me into a kiss. She kissed me hard as she moaned, "Mmm. Mmm." When our kiss broke, she said, "Slgueme molestando, estas sacando boleto." (If you keep that up, you're asking for it.)

I said to myself, "Fuck it," and then dropped to my knees in front of her. I pulled my finger out and pushed my tongue in so I could taste her sweet nectar. She tasted fruity in my mouth. As I went up and sucked her clit between my lips, she lifted her other leg and pushed my head deep into her folds.

"Si, papi, si. Tu es muy bueno," (Yes, daddy, yes, it is very good,) she cried out as I sucked her clit hard but slow. "Carajo, si papi. En la madre!" (Shit. Yes, daddy. Oh my god!) she continued to yell out as cum squirted out of her hole and coated my chin.

After she came, I stood up, and when I did, she placed her hand around my dick. Her nipples stood at attention, so I placed my mouth upon them and ran my tongue over them one by one. I then looked up at her and said, as she stroked my dick, "Damn, mami. That pussy tasted good on this tongue."

She smiled and gave me a seductive look, and then hopped off the back of the couch and dropped right to her knees and said, "Tengo una sorpresa para ti." (I have a surprise for you.)

"Oh, shit," was all I managed to say as she took my dick into her mouth slow and sensual, as if it was made of glass and was fragile. "Hell yeah. That shit feels good. Mmm hmmm, mami. Suck that dick good for me," I said as I grabbed a handful of her dark locks and twisted them between my fingers. My whole dick disappeared as she cupped my balls with her long fingernails and tickled them. "Damn, girl, you gonna make me cum too quick," I said as I began to push into her throat a little faster.

She dropped my dick from her warm mouth and said, "¿Por qué tienes tanta prisa? (Why are you in such a hurry?)

Still not understanding her, I tried to push my dick back into her mouth, but she resisted and stood up. She grabbed my hand and then walked me to my bedroom. I didn't know how she knew where it was, but who was I to protest? I wanted to get up in that foreign pussy and give it the fuck of a lifetime. I had never been with a Spanish woman, so I was excited about the experience. The lack of understanding her language was like the ultimate aphrodisiac.

When we made it to my room, she let my hand go and got on my bed, and said to me in her sweet, accented voice, "¿Crees acabar todo es trabajo?" (Think you can finish the job?) She lay back, propped her head on the pillows, and spread her legs. She took both of her hands and opened her pussy lips for me as my hard dick guided me to the bed. "No te hagas el inocente." (Don't look so innocent.)

As I walked to her, I said, "You ready for this big black dick, mami?" I stroked it as I climbed onto the bed and continued talking to her. "I'm, about to fuck that Spanish pussy real good. A nigga gonna have you talking Russian by the time it's over." I got between her legs, and before I did anything else, I leaned down and sucked her light-brown nipples one at a time as she moaned in pleasure.

"Mmm, si, papi. Si." (Mmm, yes, daddy. Yes.) I put my teeth on one and bit down lightly, pulling my head up a little as if I were trying to rip it off like a pit bull. I then did the other one the same way before coming up. I put the head of my dick at her opening and pushed it slowly inside of her wet core. I pressed hard on her clit as she told me, "No seas miserable!" (Don't be stingy!)

Somehow, I felt like she was talking shit about my slow approach, so I pushed the rest of my length inside of her. "Damn, this pussy is tight," I said to her as she brought her hands down and gripped my ass cheeks tightly. I pushed into her as she brought her hips up and met my motions.

"Si. Si. Por favor, papi. Coger mi cono bueno." (Yes. Yes. Please, daddy. Fuck my pussy good.)

She maneuvered her legs up on my shoulders into the buck position as I went deeper into her. My balls spanked her ass as my dick beat her walls. "Fuck, I'm gonna cum. This pussy is good as fuck. Shit," I cried out as my dick enjoyed what we shared together. I hoped that she would knock at my door again after this.

She removed a hand off of my ass and started masturbating her clit while she cried out and looked up at me. "Carajo, papi. Si. Si. Es muy bueno." (Shit, daddy. Yes, yes. It's so good.) I then pulled my dick out and when I did, she came up and grabbed it with her hand. She pulled it into her mouth and then reached between my legs with her other hand and pushed a manicured finger into my ass. The unexpected move caught me off guard but made my orgasm more intense.

My girl had never done no shit like that to me before, but after this experience, I just might ask her next time she sucked my dick. "Suck that dick, mami. Make me cum and swallow all of that good juice. Yeah, mami. Suck it," I said as I grabbed the back of her head and fucked her mouth until my seeds shot out and went down her throat.

When I was done, she let my dick fall from her mouth and then looked up at me and said, "Ya es tarde," (It is late,) and then proceeded to get up. She put her face in front of mine and kissed me softly on the lips.

She got off the bed and walked out of my bedroom, leaving me there on the bed still on my knees. Dick soft, balls hanging low, and confusion all in my brain. I finally got up and left the room to find her, and when I did, she was already dressed. I asked her, "You good, mami?"

As if she understood me, she nodded her pretty little head and said, "Si, necesitas algo, pegame un grito." (Yes, if you need anything, give me a yell.) She then passed me a piece of paper before she turned around and walked out, shutting the door behind her. I stood there for a few minutes because I was still dumbfounded by what took place. I finally snapped out of it and opened the piece of paper she had handed me. It had a phone number on it, no name or anything else. Perhaps she wanted to keep it that way so things wouldn't be personal between us.

I had totally forgotten about the playoff game, and when I finally remembered it, I said, "Oh shit, the game." I went and sat in front of the television, still naked from my rendezvous with the Spanish mami. I told myself that I would invest in a Spanish to English dictionary and prepare myself before I called her for a repeat.

As I watched the game, I thought about my girl and how wonderful it would be for me, her, and the Spanish mami to have a tryst. I knew my girl had a jealous streak, but it was worth a shot. I turned the game off and daydreamed about my girl getting her pussy sucked by the stranger. I grabbed my semi-hard dick and stroked it slowly as the thoughts crossed my mind. Pre-cum formed on the tip as I closed my eyes and went to another world. I saw it as clear as day. There she was, in front of me again, but this time she wasn't alone.

"Vengo a gorrearte un café," (I came to bum a cup of coffee off you,) she said with an empty cup in her hand.

My girl was behind the Spanish mami with her arms around her. She rolled her pretty brown nipples between her fingers. I jacked my dick harder. "Damn, baby, this some freaky shit," I said to my girl as she stuck her tongue out and licked the mami's neck.

She put her hand on top of the girl's head and pushed her down to her knees. My girl came around and turned her back to me while the mami spread my girl's ass cheeks. I held my dick straight up so it could slide easily into my girl's fat pussy. "Yeah, baby, get on that dick and ride it." The Spanish mami came closer and got between my girl's legs and pulled her swollen clit into her mouth.

As my girl rode my dick slow and steady, the mami in front of her sucked her hard. I felt her do that thing with her finger as it slid into my ass. She pulled it in and out as my dick played hide and seek in the wetlands. "Shit, y'all 'bout to make me cum. Go ahead, baby, ride that dick." I held onto my girl's hips as she rode me to another world.

She cried out, "I'm cumming on this dick, baby. Yes, I'm cumming." She rode me harder as I continued to watch the Spanish girl's head bob up and down with her rhythm, refusing to let go of her clit.

As my girl's white cream covered my dick, I yelled out, "I'm cumming with you. Shit." My girl hopped off my dick as the Spanish mami took it into her mouth and sucked me dry.

I was suddenly jarred out of my day dream by a knock at the door. I felt something wet and looked down. I still had my dick in my hand, and it was covered in my cum. The daydream seemed so real, and I must have jacked myself to an orgasm while I thought about my girl riding it. I knew I couldn't answer the door like this, so I hurried and got up and ran into the bathroom. The knocking continued, only this time it was much louder. I kinda hoped it would be another sweet surprise once I opened it.

After I cleaned myself off, I ran back into the living room and put my clothes on. They were still in a heap on the floor where I left them. I walked to the door as I zipped my pants up, and said out loud, "Okay, okay. I'm coming, shit." The knock came one more time before I made it to the door. When I finally yanked it open, I blinked my eyes to make sure they were not deceiving me. I finally stopped blinking and looked straight ahead into the eyes of my girl and the Spanish mami from earlier. They had their arms around each other, and I yelled out to ask, "What the fuck is going on?" I felt like I had been duped, and that what happened earlier was all planned.

They both looked at me as the mami said in her deep accent, "Yo quiero mi café' conpiquete," (I want a shot of liquor in my coffee) and then they walked inside and shut the door behind them.

Chapter Six

Unexpected Pleasure

My dick was so hard it looked like it was about to burst. My balls were filled to capacity and needed a release. My bitch was nowhere in sight and wouldn't be for a few more days. I said to myself, "Fuck it," and then put my hand around my dick shaft and stroked slowly. "Shit. I need to fuckin' cum," I said aloud as I stroked a little faster. The pre-cum on the tip of my dick shined like a diamond in the bright sun. Jacking my dick wasn't going to work because my shit needed to be up in something warm to reach the pleasure it sought. I had never thought about cheating on my bitch before because her pussy and head game had always been on point but damn, what else was a nigga to do?

I tried to think about my girl's wet pussy and gripped my dick harder. My nut sack bounced up and down with each thrust of my hand. "Damn. A nigga needs some pussy," I said out loud, as if my bitch was lying there beside me and I was letting her know it. I looked over at her side of the bed as if she would magically appear, but I knew that would not happen. The weekend was three days away but felt like a lifetime. I knew that I should have gotten enough pussy to last me until she got back, but even that may not have stopped my dick from needing another release.

"I cant do this shit," I stated angrily, as I let my dick fall from my hand. It was so hard that the impact of it hitting the bottom of my stomach actually stung a little. I got up out of the bed with my dick and nuts swinging side to side. My dick hit my thighs, as if punishing me for not carrying through and fulfilling its needs. I decided a cold shower would probably be best. I hoped it would soothe the throbbing inside of my nut sack.

As soon as I turned the shower water on, I heard the door-bell ring. "Who the fuck could be at my damn door?" I asked out loud. I turned the water back off and grabbed a towel, wrapping it around my waist, and went to see who was trying to disturb my peace. I didn't even ask who was behind it when I got there because I honestly didn't give a fuck. All I knew was that somebody was about to get cursed the fuck out. I was already pissed off about my dick situation, so I would take my anger out on whoever it was.

I went completely still. This bitch knew that my girl was out of town on a work assignment, so she had no business popping up here. "What's up, Keisha? You know Tracey's out of town, so what the fuck you doing here?" I said to her with a slight attitude while looking her up and down. I never really cared for her, but the bitch was fine. She also had on very little clothing, revealing skin I shouldn't have been looking at.

I could feel my dick begin to rise once again as she spoke, "I know she gone, but damn. I'm bored as fuck." She looked from my eyes to the towel around my waist. My dick had started to grow and formed a bump in front of the towel. I put my hand in front of it and tried to push my dick down, but that motherfucker wanted some pussy, and there was nothing I could do to tame him. Keisha laughed and started swaying her body from side to side, and then asked, "Why don't you just go ahead and let me in? You look like you need some com-pany."

My mouth tried to form the word no, but my dick took control and said yes. I quickly blurted out, "Yeah. I guess I could use a little company, but don't come in here on no bull-shit." I opened the door up wide enough for her to walk past me and when she did, the back side of her hand brushed across my dick. I backed up a little, trying to maintain what little bit of composure I had left. I closed the door back and locked it as I watched her switch her wide hips over to the couch and sit down. I could see her braless nipples pop out of her sleeveless tank top, as if they were watching me and waiting to see what I would do. The tennis skirt was really short and barely covered her fat ass. I could see her ass cheeks trying to escape from the bottom of it. When she sat down on the couch, she spread her thick thighs just enough for me to see the wet spot that had formed on her thongs. I shook my head and said to her, "Chill the fuck out, Keish, 'cause ain't shit going down in here." I then turned to go back to the bathroom so I could get decent. I locked the door behind me just in case her ass wanted to try something slick. I knew I might be in trouble if I didn't.

I took a quick rinse off and went to put my pants on, forgetting that I had left them in the bedroom. I put the towel back around my waist and went to retrieve my jeans. When I walked in my bedroom, Keisha was sitting on the edge of the bed with her legs crossed and her nipples still at attention. I stopped in my tracks and then put my hands on my hips before I said to her, "Yo, Keish, get the fuck outta here with that bullshit. I already told you that ain't shit going down up in here."

She looked at me seductively and then crossed her legs. The wet spot on her thongs was bigger now from the moisture her pussy was emitting. She said to me, "You can't tell me that you ain't been wanting to get up in this fat pussy." She then pulled the thongs to the side after opening her legs wider. "I know you see this fat pussy all in your face. Nigga, you know you want some," she said as she stood up and pulled her thongs all the way off. She then dropped her skirt and pulled the tank top over her head. My dick reacted no matter how hard I tried to contain it.

The hardness pushed against the towel, trying to get loose as Keisha sat back on the bed. She pulled up both of her legs and spread them as wide as she could. Her fat clit pushed out from between her pussy lips. She was making it hard for a nigga to maintain, but I held steady. "What's the matter? You ain't never seen a pussy this fat before?" she asked hungrily as her finger found her clit. My dick steady tried to break through the barrier of the towel holding it back.

Keisha got up and repositioned herself on her elbows and knees. Her fat ass spread like the Red Sea as her pussy juice shimmered in the dim lighting. I finally spoke again, "Yo, shut that shit down and get the fuck outta here." I then tried to turn around and walk out of the room, but my dick would not let me do it.

Keisha brought her small hand between her legs and pushed a finger into her pussy. "Come on and put something inside this wet pussy. Tracey said the dick was good, but I'm not sure I believe her," she said as she pushed her finger in and out, coating it with her juices.

"Damn," I said, mainly to myself. I needed to cum bad, and I had one of two options. Fuck the wet pussy in front of me, or turn around and walk the hell out.

I must have been in a deep trance, because I didn't remember seeing Keisha get off the bed and walking over to me. I snapped out of it when I felt the towel drop from around my waist. As the cool breeze hit my dick, I looked down and into Keisha's eyes. She was on her knees in front of me about to put my dick in her mouth. As soon as the head of it disappeared, all thoughts of my girl were gone. "Oh shit. Damn, that feels good," I said out loud as I allowed Keisha to do what she wanted. When she cupped my balls in her hand, I squeezed my ass cheeks together trying to keep from cumming too soon.

I knew that I was dead ass wrong for this, but the way she rolled her tongue over my dick head had my knees about to buckle. "Shit, Keish, that feels so good. Hell yeah," I said to her as her big lips wrapped around my dick and made it disappear.

She reached her hands around and squeezed my ass while she sucked me hard and slow. "Mmm, mmm, hmmm," she moaned as her spit covered the skin of my dick. I fucked her mouth harder and faster as she moved her hands from my ass to my balls and then pressed on them like she could push the cum out of me.

"Yeah, suck that dick. Damn, that shit feels good. Yes, Keish. Make my dick cum for you." She let my balls go and then twisted her nipples. Not even a minute later, she let my dick fall from her mouth. I was on the verge of cumming, so I asked, irritated, "Yo, what the fuck you doing?"

I watched her get up off her knees and walk back to the bed I shared with my bitch. She got on it and positioned herself on her hands and knees again and said, "I didn't come over here to suck dick. I'm trying to get stuffed with that motherfucker." She ran a finger down the middle of her pussy lips and then put the tip inside. I started to walk over to her but stopped when she removed her hand and turned over. She reached over to my girl's nightstand and pulled the drawer open.

When I saw her pull out a dildo, I just had to ask, "How the fuck did you know that was there?"

She shut the drawer and answered, "Nigga, me and Tracey been fucking for the longest. She said I fucked her better than you. You gonna prove her wrong?"

Shocked, I asked, "What the fuck did you say?" I was surprised and not sure if I believed her not. "Bitch, get the fuck outta here with that bullshit," I said to her, feeling slightly angry at the comment.

Keisha put the dildo in her mouth and sucked it like a real dick. It caused me to forget all about the comment she had just made. I started stroking my dick faster. I was gonna fuck the shit out of this bitch for trying me. "Come on, you know you wanna fuck this pussy hard. Come knock these walls down," she said when she pulled the dildo from her mouth. She then put it between her legs and pushed it into her pussy, coating it with her juices.

I knew that I was about to commit the ultimate sin, but I could no longer contain myself. Her pussy was fat and juicy. As my dick led the way, the pre-cum formed. "Damn, girl. Let a nigga taste that pussy first," I said to her as I licked my lips and went down on my knees.

She pulled the dildo out and ran it over her clit. She then reached out to hand it to me and said, "You can suck this pussy, but I want you to fuck me in the ass with this while you do it." She licked her lips and added, "That's the type of shit I like."

I took the cum-coated dildo from her hand and put into her asshole and said, "You a freaky bitch. Trace don't ever let me do no shit like this."

She pinched her nipples and said seductively, "You can do whatever you want. I just want to be fucked real good and hard." I slowly pushed the dildo into her asshole as the cum from her pussy ran down the little space between the two holes. "Yes, that's it. Don't go so slow. Fuck this ass like a beast," she called out as I sped up. I then bent over a little and took her swollen clit into my mouth. She had a sweet fruity flavor and it made me suck harder as I continued to fuck her in the ass. "Yes, oh god. Fuck yes. Make this pussy cum again. Yes, yes," she cried out, and then put both of her hands on the back of my head and pushed my face into her. She brought her ass up to meet the rhythm of the dildo, as I pondered once again on what she said about her and Tracey. In a way, I hoped it was true because I wouldn't mind having both of them sucking my dick while I played in their pussies. "I'm cumming. Yes, yes, oh yes, I'm cumming," she yelled out as her milky cream coated my chin. I sucked her clit until I thought she was done, and was now more than ready to stick pipe to her. I was gonna fuck this bitch so good. She would dream about me at night.

I pulled the dildo out of her ass and told her, "Turn that ass over. Let a nigga all the way in there." She looked at me through squinted eyes and then did as I said. Before she turned over, she reached a hand up and pulled on my balls. When she turned completely over, I didn't waste any time. I spread her open and pushed my nine inches into her. I gripped her ass cheeks and my nails dug into her meaty flesh. My thoughts of Tracey were gone as I went balls deep into her ocean. "Damn, girl, this pussy good. I'm gonna fuck this pussy right. You gonna be begging for this dick," I said to her in between thrusts. I pushed a thumb into her asshole and continued ranting. "Tell me you like this dick, Keisha. Push that pussy back on it and wet this dick up."

She gripped the sheets with one hand and masturbated her clit with the other as she called out in pleasure, "This dick is good, motherfucker. Fuck this pussy. Make this pussy cum all over that dick. Oh yes. Yes. Fuck me harder."

Our bodies slammed into each other so loud I was sure the neighbors heard us. I could feel myself about to cum and said to Keisha, "Get up and come swallow these seeds. I'm about to cum. This good pussy is about to make me cum." About that time, I heard a door slam behind me. My seeds slithered back into their shell as if running away. My dick fell out of the pussy and shriveled up like it had done nothing wrong. I turned around and looked into my woman's eyes.

"Nigga, don't stop because of me. Keep fucking that good ass pussy like I ain't here," Tracey said with her hands on her hips. I looked like a deer caught in headlights and couldn't form any words to save myself.

Keisha spoke instead, "It's about damn time you got here. You been missing out on all the fun." She smiled at my girl and continued, "His scary ass almost didn't give in, but this pussy talked him into it." They shared a laugh, but I didn't find shit funny.

I asked both of them, "What the fuck is going on here? Y'all bitches on some bullshit."

Tracey walked over to the bed where Keisha was still on her hands and knees and pushed a finger into her pussy. She turned to me and said, "Get yourself together, baby. This pussy was so good to me that I just had to share it with you."

She then pulled her finger out and put it in her mouth to suck the juices off of it. Tracey dropped her dress as Keisha turned over on her back. When she bent over in between Keisha's thighs, my dick begin to grow again. "Damn, baby, why you been holding out on me? How long this shit been going on?"

The sounds of my girl eating the pussy in front of her made my mouth water. I got behind Tracey and did to her what I did to Keisha earlier. I rammed my dick in like I was angry, and in a way, I guess I was. Tracey sucked Keisha's pussy into another orgasm as I fucked her like never before.

When Keisha was done cumming, she got up from under Tracey and grabbed the dildo. She then straddled Tracey's back while facing me. As she looked me in the eyes, she pushed the rubber dick into my girl's ass. Tracey cried out in pleasure, "Yes. Yes. Mmm, fuck me good. Yes, oh, oh, yeah."

As I fucked her pussy and her friend fucked her ass, Keisha pulled my tongue into her mouth and sucked it. My girl yelled out after only a couple of minutes, "I'm fucking cumming. Oh yes, please don't stop now. Shit. I'm cumming."

Her cum began to cover my dick and no sooner than I felt it, I was ready to cum too. I pulled my tongue from Keisha's mouth and said, "This dick's about to cum. What y'all bitches gonna do?" Keisha smiled a toothy smile and got up from over Tracey's back. When she pulled my dick out of her pussy, my cum shot out like a water gun.

Tracey got up and turned around so she and her friend could drink my cum together. They pressed on my balls as they cleaned my dick up. The unexpected treat was amazing, and I hoped that it would happen again soon. When we were done, I lay back on the pillows as they each got under an arm and laid their heads on my chest. I put an arm around each one of them and drifted off to sleep with the two women nestled beside me.

I didn't know how long I had been asleep, but I woke up to my nipples being sucked on. Tracey massaged my balls in her hand as Keisha stroked my dick with hers. "Now this is how a nigga should wake up every day," I said out loud to them. They let my shit go and got up on their knees and faced each other with me still between them. I could see their fat clits poking out, and as they kissed, I pinched each one between my thumb and forefinger. I pulled on their clits really hard as my dick rose to attention again. I pushed a finger into each of their pussies as they gyrated their hips and rode. I finally said, "Come on and let a nigga get an early morning nut. Y'all bitches are being greedy now."

They stopped kissing, and as Keisha turned and straddled me backward, my dick slid right into her. Tracey turned and straddled my face with her overnight essence. The scent of her marinated pussy juice had me ready to bust. I could feel the pressure of Keisha's hands on my thighs as she rode my dick like a polo champ. I wanted to watch my dick slide in and out of the pussy, but Tracey's fat pussy lips had me blinded. I could hear the moisture of the pussy that I was inside of, even over the moans of the two women.

"Mmm hmmm."

"Oh god, yes."

"Suck this pussy, baby."

"Yes, oh yes."

Then both of them yelled out at the same time, "Oh my god, I'm cumming."

"Fuck, I'm cumming."

I felt one's wetness on my chin and the other one's wetness on my pelvic area as they came.

When they were done, they both got up. Keisha came up and sucked the cum off my lips and chin as Tracey went down and sucked it off of my dick. Then they looked at each other and giggled. Once I was cleaned up, they got up and began to put their clothes back on. I asked, "What the fuck is going on? Hell no, I know y'all ain't gonna leave me hanging like this." They continued getting dressed as if I hadn't said shit. I finally got up off the bed, frustrated, with my dick still hard, and said, "Y'all come on and get this dick right. How y'all gonna cum and forget about me? What the fuck is up with that?" I steady stroked my dick as I talked to them, but they ignored me. "This is some flaw ass shit y'all got going on," I said, but they continued to ignore me as if I hadn't spoken at all. When they were done dressing, they turned around and walked out.

When the door slammed behind them, I opened my eyes and heard someone knocking. I looked down and saw my dick in my hand with my cum all over me. "What the fuck?" I asked myself. I must have been dreaming the whole scenario that had just taken place. "Hell nah, that shit was too real," I said out loud as I heard the knock again. I let go of my dick and yelled out, "Hold the fuck on. I'll be there in a second." I ran into the bathroom and grabbed a towel. Before wrapping it around my waist, I wiped off as much of my cum as I could. I then secured the towel and went to answer the door. The person behind it was knocking harder now. I undid the lock and yanked the door open. "Damn, who the fuck....?"

I looked into Keisha's eyes as she said, "You look like you could use some company."

Chapter Seven

Paradise Found

Walking up to him every morning was like waking up in paradise. His perfectly formed body was so beautifully sculpted, like a statue. Each line and crevice were exactly where it was supposed to be. The dark-brown pigment of his skin was like freshly poured chocolate. His man nipples were just the right size on his chiseled chest. His face was so handsome it should have been on the cover of *GQ* magazine every month the issue came out. His lips were plump and smooth, covering his perfectly aligned teeth. His tongue, oh my god, his tongue. Long and fat. The things it was capable of were beyond extraordinary. Just the mere thought of it made my pussy wet.

As I laid there and admired him, he continued to sleep so peacefully. His long lashes were like little butterflies perched in the trees, wanting to flutter away but waiting for the perfect gust of wind to do so. I didn't ever want to leave the spot beside him because I couldn't think of anywhere else I'd rather be. I tried hard to hold back from touching him but when I was close to him, it was hard to keep my composure. I took my long, manicured nail and ran it along the lines of his skin. He stirred, and I stopped when he turned on his side. His back now faced me as his ass touched my leg. I wasn't going to let him get away that easy, though.

I reached up and ran that same nail down his spine until I made it to the crack of his ass. As I ran it down the length of his crack, he stirred again but, this time, he spoke, "What you looking for back there? You need some help?"

I smiled and continued my attack. When I reached the end of his crack, I slid my finger in the middle of it and touched his asshole. I then responded, "Mmm. Don't worry. I already found what I was looking for."

After I explored the outside of it, I gently pushed my small finger into the hole. "Ah, shit," he said as I pulled out and then pushed back in.

"I woke up so fucking wet and horny, baby," I said to him hungrily as I put my lips to the back of his neck. I pulled my finger out so I could explore him further.

I found his balls and kneaded them like homemade biscuits I was preparing to bake. They were full of what I desired and it made me thirsty. He asked as he continued to lay there, still and waiting for my next move, "What you gonna do with those?"

I didn't respond just yet. Instead, I rose and turned my body the other way so that I could be up close and personal with the only thing that could quench my thirst. I then said, "I'm gonna juice these like oranges and make me something to drink."

He stayed with his back to me, and when I stuck out my tongue and licked his thigh, he flinched. "Damn, baby," he stated as I traced the roundness of each one of his balls. He then lifted his leg and turned over. He rested that leg on the other side of me and now straddled my face and neck. I took a ball into my mouth and sucked it like a sucker. I pretended it was a blow pop and I was trying to get to the fruity bubble gum in the middle. "Mmm hmmm. That shit feels good," he said as I closed my eyes. I loved to make him moan and feel good. When I opened my eyes, I met his as they stared down at me. I was ready to swallow some of his sweet juice, so I let his balls go and got up.

As I maneuvered from under his leg, I felt him run a finger over my skin and it sent chill bumps down my spine. I got up on my knees between his legs and looked him up and down.

The little eye on the head of his dick looked back at me. The pre-cum looked like a gem glaring into my eyes. He spoke again, "You just gonna look at it, or you gonna do something with it?" I said nothing as I ran my finger up his length. It was long and thick and appeared to be too much for my small frame. However, it was just enough to fill up my walls.

I ran my fingertip over the hole and then wrapped the rest of my fingers around him. The clear liquid that had formed now smeared over the tip of it. "Damn, baby, you know just how to tease me," he said as he reached his hand down to meet mine. He covered my small hand with his and left mine there to complete the task. Both of his legs bent at the knees and spread wide so I could get to every corner of him.

I bent down, and as I held onto his thickness with one hand, I lifted his balls with the other. I stuck my tongue out and traced his asshole as he moaned in pleasure, "Mmm hmmm. Yeah, baby. You know I love that shit." I only pleasured it for a few seconds and then came back up to my paradise. I traced the head of his dick with my tongue and then wrapped my lips around it. I sucked it hard as he thrusted his lips lightly to meet my tongue. He grabbed a handful of my hair and pulled hard. The sudden pain filled me with extra pleasure and caused me to suck harder. My cheeks sunk in as his thickness filled my mouth. "Damn, that feels good. Suck this dick, baby, suck that shit like I like it," he said as he thrusted harder into me. I opened my eyes and cut them up at him as he said, "Turn around so I can suck that pussy."

I loved it when he got nasty, so I lifted myself toward him. When I straddled his chest, he immediately reached up and spread my ass cheeks. He stuck his nose up to my pussy hole and smelled my morning wetness and said, "This pussy smells so damn good. I'm about to eat this shit for breakfast." He then stuck his tongue out and reached my clit.

I bucked a little and moaned, "Mmm, mmm." As he flicked his tongue over my pearl, I swallowed the dick. I sucked him hard and when I felt a finger go in my pussy, I went faster.

As he finger-fucked me, he licked my asshole and made me thrust against him slowly. I grinded my ass into his face, and it was a miracle that he could even breathe. I let his dick go and said, "Baby, you gonna make me cum." He pulled his finger from my pussy and replaced it with his tongue. He then gripped my clit between his thumb and forefinger and pulled. "Mmm hmmm," I moaned as I prepared myself for an eruption. I sucked his dick faster now and kneaded his balls at the same time. Suddenly, I stiffened and had to let the dick go again. "I'm cumming. Fuck. Baby, I'm cumming," I yelled out as much as I could and I went back to sucking him.

After I finished cumming, he slapped me on the ass and pushed me up. He then said, "Come on and let me get up in this pussy."

I dropped his dick from my hand and got off him and asked, "How do you want it, daddy?" I looked at him innocently, although, deep inside of me, it had been hard waiting for it.

He reached out and pinched my nipples hard, leaving them throbbing. "Boot that ass up. I'm trying to go deep in that pussy."

I giggled excitedly as I positioned myself on my elbows and knees. I then arched my back deeply so my ass would be high. He decided to stand, so he got up and stood on the side of the bed and turned to me. The floor would help him keep a steady balance so he could go deep in the pussy and fuck me harder. "Ugh, oh, baby," I said as he gripped my hips with his strong hands.

I could feel his nails dig into my flesh as he positioned the head of his dick at my opening. "You ready for this dick?" he asked as the head suddenly crept into my cave.

I answered him hungrily, "Yes, baby. Please give me the dick. This pussy is so ready for it. Please fuck me good with it." He pushed the head in and then pulled it out making my wet pussy pop. "Oh shit," I said out loud. I was a little pissed because I wanted the whole dick up in me and he was teasing me with it instead. He pushed just the head in again, and I said, "Stop teasing me and fuck this pussy."

I heard him laugh lightly, and then he said, "Oh, you telling me what to do now? I'm gonna have to punish you for that shit."

He pushed his dick into me hard and almost made me lose my breath. His balls bounced up and hit my clit, leaving it stinging. "Oh god, yes," I said as I waited for his next move.

He leaned over with his dick still inside of me and then reached around to grab my nipples. As he pinched and pulled them, he said in a stern voice, "This is my pussy and I fuck it when I want and how I want. Do you understand?"

I loved it when he got aggressive while he fucked me. I answered him while my nipples ached between his fingers. "Yes, yes, I understand. It's your pussy, daddy. It's all yours."

He pulled my nipples one last time and then let them go. They still stung long after, trying to recover from his torture. He pulled his dick out and stopped when he got to the head, still teasing me. When he pushed it back in, he demanded, "Play with that clit while I fuck this pussy and make it cum."

I reached a hand down between my legs to do as he told me. I placed my middle finger over my clit and started going back and forth masturbating it. He sped up as he pulled out and pushed in. His pelvis slammed into me hard, causing my ass cheeks to move in waves. "Yes, baby. Yes. Fuck me. Fuck your pussy and make this bitch cum," I cried out in pleasure.

He then asked, "Do you like how this dick is beating that pussy up? Huh? Tell me. Tell me how much you like this dick." I ignored him because I knew that if I didn't answer him right away, he would punish me and fuck me harder. He slapped me on the ass really hard and said, "You gonna ignore me now? Huh? You better tell me how this dick feels to you before I take it out of this pussy."

The fear of him pulling out made me answer him, "Yes, yes. Oh my god, I love this dick. It feels so good inside of me."

I felt him pull out and rub his dick along my ass crack, coating it with my pussy juice. He then pushed it back inside of me as he rubbed my juice in with his thumb, and then it entered me. His thumb was long and fat, and as it filled my asshole, I felt myself about to cum. "I'm gonna cum all over this dick. Yes, baby, I'm about to cum, so please don't stop." I masturbated my clit a little faster as he continued to fuck me hard.

He then said, "That's right, go ahead and cum on this dick. Cover this motherfucker with that cream. Come on, baby. Cum for me."

As my cum squirted out on him, I had to stop masturbating because I had to grip the sheets to maintain my control. The force of the orgasm was so intense I thought I would faint right then and there. "Oh, oh, oh my god. Oh my god. Yes, yes, yes," I steady cried.

As he slowed his rhythm, he said, "Now it's my turn to cum. You ready for this?" He pulled his dick out of my pussy and made me flip over on my back. He then put my legs up over his shoulders, and as he looked me deeply in the eyes, he pushed his dick back inside of me.

The force of his entry made it feel like he had never been inside of me. He pushed my legs back to my chest as far as he could get them and fucked me deep, so deep. I swear I could feel him in my chest. "You gonna take every inch of this dick until you make it cum," he said to me as his balls fell between my ass cheeks. I played with my stiffened nipples as he plunged in and out of me. Then, suddenly, he blurted out, "Shit. I'm about to cum." He only gave a few more strokes and then pulled out. He held his dick in his hand and stroked back and forth as his cum shot out all over my breasts and stomach.

As he slowed down, I took my hands and rubbed his liquid essence into my skin. I then licked my fingers so I could taste his creamy cum. "Mmm hmmm. This shit tastes so good. I gotta have some more of this," I said to him seductively.

He then asked me, "Well, what you gonna do to get it?"

As he let his dick go and smiled at me, I scooted my body back so I could sit up, and said, "Yeah. I'm about to show you what I'm gonna do."

He put both of his hands on my head as I gripped his semi-hard dick in my hand and slowly stroked it so I could bring it back to life. "Yeah, that feels good," he said as he rocked his hips in time to the rhythm of my hand. He leaned his head back in pleasure as I continued to stroke him. "Mmm hmm, yeah, baby. Come on and wake that dick back up," he said greedily as I ran my tongue over the tip of him. I reached my free hand between his legs, causing him to spread them slightly apart. When he did, I pushed my hand under his balls and found his asshole. I loved to play with his little hole because it took him to another level of ecstasy. I pressed on the hole and then lightly traced it with my finger. I pulled my hand back from under his nuts and put it between my legs. "Yeah, baby. It's getting back right just for you. Suck this dick. Yes," he cried out in pleasure as I sucked the head of his dick hard.

I pushed the finger I just had at his hole into my wet pussy and coated it with my juices. I went in and out a few times before pulling it all the way out and then back under his nut sack. I stuck it to his asshole again, but instead of just circling it, I pushed my cum-coated finger inside. "Holy shit, mmm hmmm. Damn, baby. You know just what to do to make a nigga feel good. Yes." He pushed on my head harder now as I pushed my finger in and out of him. His asshole was nice and tight and sucked my finger right in.

His dick was back hard now and hit the back of my throat like it was a battering ram trying to bust a door open. I relaxed my gag reflexes and could feel it go down as far as it could reach. I dropped my hand from around it so I could take all of it, and not even a minute later, he cried out in his sexy bedroom voice, "Keep sucking, I'm about to cum. Suck it harder, baby, I'm cumming. Shit, I'm cumming." I could feel his muscles stiffen, and as his asshole tightened even more around my finger, the vein in his dick began to pulse as if it was going into cardiac arrest. "Oh yes, yes. Shit," he yelled as his delicious juices shot out and slid down my throat. I continued to suck him until he was drained, and then I pulled my finger out. Before I pulled my hand all the way out from between his legs, I gripped his balls and massaged them, making sure they had given all they could.

His grip on my head lessened as his dick began to shrink. I finally let him fall from my mouth and then kissed the tip of the head and asked, "You good now?"

He ran his fingers through my hair and said, "Damn right, you always on point when it comes to this dick." He leaned down and kissed me gently on the lips and then grabbed my hand and said, "Come on, baby. Let's go get cleaned up."

I didn't protest, because I knew that once we got in the shower, our paradise would be found and explored again.

Sugar E. Walls

Chapter Eight

A Wild Ride

As he whipped and wheeled through the heavy traffic, the vibrations from the road below had my clit throbbing. My pussy was getting oh so wet, and I swear I could feel myself about to cum right there in my seat. The heat that I felt in my body had me sweating, although the vents blew cool air out onto me. We still had a couple of hours to go before we reached our destination, but I didn't think I'd be able to wait that long.

I reached my left arm over and brushed my hand over his waves. He was so focused on his mission that he really didn't pay me much attention, but I'd be damned if I let him ignore me. I ran my manicured nails down the side of his face and then across his mouth. Once my finger touched his lips, he gave it a small kiss and then he put his concentration back on the road. I finally told him, "Oh, baby, I am so fucking horny right now."

He turned his handsome face to me and told me in a disappointing voice, "Just hold on a little longer, baby. You know yo' nigga got you as soon as we get to the motel." I refused to settle for his response, because I needed to cum right then and I was not going to wait.

"Uh, uh. This pussy needs to be touched right now. She ain't waiting for nothing," I said to him hungrily as I kicked my sandals off. I then continued, "The fuck you mean you got me when we get to the motel? Nah, nigga, I need you to get me now."

I then pulled my shorts down and over my feet. I didn't have any panties on, so that was one less thing for me to worry about. When he noticed what I had done, he asked, "Baby, what the hell you doing?" He swerved a little and then put his eyes back on the road. Little did he know, my pussy was going to cum with or without him.

I lifted my legs and turned in my seat and then rested my back against the passenger side door. I then said to him, "Don't you wanna pull over for just a minute? Come on, baby, I'm so fucking horny it ain't gonna take me but a minute. Please, baby, I need to cum so bad." I then spread my legs and used my fingers to spread my pussy lips open wide.

"Baby, you know we got to be there on time. If we stop, we ain't gonna make it," he said to me as he licked his luscious lips. The same lips that I wanted on my wet pussy. He was playing hard to get, but I wouldn't stop until I had his dick deep inside of me.

I pulled the hood back on my clit and my little pearl popped right out. I said to him seductively, "Now you know you wanna suck on this fat clit, baby."

He lifted his eyebrows and licked his lips again as I pressed down on my clit and rotated my finger in circular motions. "Come on now, you really gonna do me like that?" he stated as I pushed the tip of my finger into my dripping wet hole.

When I pulled it out, I got up and crawled over to him, putting my finger under his nose, and said, "Smell that pussy juice, baby. Don't you wanna wear it like it's cologne?"

He reached his free hand up and grabbed my hand. He then opened his mouth and sucked that same finger, tasting my essence. As he sucked the juice off it, he moaned, "Mmm, mmm. Damn, you taste so sweet." I reached my hand down and undid his Dickies as he asked, "What you about to do down there?"

I pulled his semi-hard dick out and kissed him on the cheek before I responded, "I'm thirsty, so I'm about to suck my favorite drink out of this motherfucker." I put my head down in between his body and the steering wheel and found my favorite place on earth.

"Holy shit," he stated as he gripped the wheel with both hands.

I sucked the head of his dick into my warm mouth and felt the car speed up a little. "Damn, baby, that feels good," he said as I let the rest of him meet with the back of my throat.

My spit made his length wet as I slurped and sucked him a little faster. "Slurp, slurp, slurp." The sounds of pleasure filled the quietness that had formed around us in the car. He removed one of his hands from the steering wheel and reached over to my ass and grabbed it. He then slid his middle finger down the crack of it until he found my asshole. "Mmm, sllp. Sllp. Mmm," I moaned from the feeling as I continued to suck him.

He moved from my asshole and went down a little further. He pressed hard on the small space that stretched between my two holes. It was slippery from my wetness, and him pressing down on it only made me wetter. I let his dick fall from the suction of my mouth long enough to tell him, "Mmm, baby. That feels so good," and then I put him back in between my lips and sucked even harder.

He slid his finger into my pussy hole and swirled it like he was stirring a pot of honey and coated it with my juices. "Damn, baby, this pussy is good and wet," he said as he pulled his finger out and went further to find my clit, and then he said, "You gonna fuck around and make a nigga be all late and shit. Damn."

I once again loosened up on his dick and let it fall out of my mouth. As I put my hand around it and continued to stroke it, I told him, "Pull over and hit this pussy one time real quick. Come on, baby, I know you can spare a few minutes." I knew that this job interview was big for him, but I also knew that the company wanted him really bad and being a few minutes late wouldn't change that. I only needed a second of his time, and I wouldn't stop until I got it.

His seat was pushed far enough back for me to fit between him and the steering wheel, so I took advantage of it. I grabbed his arm and pulled it from between my legs and when I did, he asked, "What's up, baby? I'm trying to make this pussy cum for you."

I looked at him like he was crazy, because he already knew that when my pussy called, it would keep calling until he dick answered. I said to him, "Nigga, you done lost your damn mind if you think I done changed mine." I got up so I could reposition myself and said, "This dick is going in this pussy one way or the other."

I started to straddle him, and he said, "What the fuck? You gonna make me wreck this damn car."

I giggled at his comment but proceeded with what I was about to do. Once my legs were in position, I put one hand on his headrest and the other one around his dick. "Just keep driving this car, baby, because I'm gonna drive this one while you do," I told him as I lifted up a little and put the head of his dick at my wet opening. I then came down, and he disappeared inside of me. "Uh, yes. Finally," I said out loud after he was completely engulfed in my walls.

The windows were tinted, so I wasn't worried about anyone seeing us. However, it wouldn't have mattered because I was getting some of this dick no matter who could see it. The thrill of the cars and trucks passing by us gave me a sudden rush of excitement. "Oh, baby, I needed this dick so bad. Yes," I cried out as I slowly pushed my body up and then down.

He tried his best to concentrate on driving, but I had the kind of pussy that would make any man lose all train of thought. "Damn, that pussy feels good on this dick," he said to me as he placed a hand on my ass.

"You like how this pussy feels sucking all up on your dick? Huh?" I asked him, because I wanted him to talk shit back to me.

"Yeah, baby, you know I love it when you ride my shit like that. Make that pussy cum for me. Cum all over this dick for daddy," he stated as he squeezed my ass cheeks really hard. His grip caused a small surge of pain that brought me even more pleasure. I reached a hand down from the head rest to between my legs and pressed really hard on my clit, building up the pressure that I wanted so bad to release. "Cum for me, baby. Cum for me, yes. Mmm hmmm," he said in a seductive whisper.

I started moving my finger up and down while still pressing on it. It felt like my pussy was now holding back and fighting to keep my cum inside, but I needed the release and wasn't nothing going to stop me from getting it. "Ooh, ooh god, yes. Oh my god, I wanna cum so bad," I cried out, pissed because I was having such a hard time when it should have been so easy.

"What's the matter, baby? That pussy being stubborn? Huh? What you need me to do for you?" he asked as I felt the car begin to slow.

I couldn't see what was going on in front of us because I had my back to the road, but I felt it when the car veered in another direction. "Oh, baby, I wanna cum so bad. I think I want it too bad," I told him as I continued to jack my swollen bud, and then I added, "I think I need you to suck on it, baby, yeah. I bet this pussy will cum for you then." I smiled and moved my hand from between my legs. I ran the tip of my finger over his lips and said, "These right here are what I need. You gonna suck this pussy for me?"

I felt it when he turned again, and then he said, "I'm about to take care of it for you. Don't worry, I got you. Daddy's gonna make that pussy squirt."

I felt the car come to a complete stop and turned my head to see what was going on. He had pulled into a motel parking lot and backed into a parking space that was located all the way in the back. I asked, "Baby, do you really have the time to get a room?"

He shook his head and responded, as he turned off the motor, "Nah, in the back seat. I'ma teach your ass to fuck with me." He put a hand on each side of my waist and helped me lift up off of him. His dick fell out of me, still nice and hard, and I couldn't wait for him to put it back in. I knew he was gonna punish me for making him have to stop and do this, and that was exactly what I wanted. "Get yo' ass in the back seat and open that pussy up for me," he demanded in a stern voice. I didn't hesitate or say anything back to him. I just did as he told me to because I had been begging for the dick.

I climbed through the front seats and into the back as quickly as I could, and then he slid in right behind me. I lay down on the seat and spread my legs. I don't know where it came from, but I suddenly felt nervous about being here doing this in an open parking lot. As soon as I felt his finger enter me, though, all the nervousness left my mind. "You gonna pay for making me have to do this," he said as he moved his finger in and out of me.

I could hear the juices moving around with every thrust of his limb. "You hear that pussy talking to you? She gets wet just for you," I said to him as I put my hand over his and pushed with him.

He looked me in the eyes and asked, "What you want a nigga to do to this pussy?"

I pulled his hand out and put it to my mouth. I then stuck the finger he had inside of me between my lips and sucked my juice off it, and then said to him, "Mmm, this some sweet pussy juice. You wanna try a little bit?" I stuck my finger in his mouth, and he sucked on it as I pulled it back.

He then bent lower and put his head in between my thighs, and before he sucked my clit into his mouth, he said, "Girl, you already know that's my favorite flavor."

The pressure from his mouth caused me to flinch and lift my legs up a little more. I put both of my hands on the back of his head and grinded my hips into him. "Oh, baby, yes, that feels good. Yes, mmm hmmm. Go ahead and make this pussy cum," I cried out to him as he continued to suck on my womanhood. I could feel myself on the verge of cumming and let him know it. "You about to make me cum, yes, oh yes. This is what I been waiting on. Oh my god, yes." He slid his finger back into me as he sucked, and when he did, my cum squirted out on it. "Yes. Yes, I'm cumming," I hollered out as I pushed his head into me harder. He continued to suck my clit until I was done.

When he finally came up for air, he pulled his pants down further and positioned his dick head at my wet hole and asked me, "Are you ready for this dick?"

I smiled at him seductively and answered, "Yes, I been ready for that dick. I want it to tear this pussy up. Punish it for making you late." As soon as I said it, he pushed his length and width into me really hard. "Ugh, shit," I blurted out as he pushed and pulled in and out of me. I grabbed his ass cheeks as he slammed into me so hard my head was hitting the door. However, it felt too good to stop him. I loved it when fucked me like that.

He started to talk shit in between strokes, "I'm...gonna...fuck the...shit...outta this...pussy. You gonna learn...to fuck...with me...when I'm on...a...mission." He then pulled out and lifted my legs higher and pushed himself into my asshole.

The sudden intrusion caught me off guard and hurt a little, but I let him do his thing without interruption. As his balls slapped me and his dick pounded into me, I cried out in pleasure, "Yes, yes, baby. Fuck me harder. Fuck this ass harder. Yes."

It only took him a few more strokes, and then he pulled out and came all over my pussy. He stroked his dick until it was empty, and then he pulled his pants up and crawled back between the seats. I laid there for a minute because I had to catch my breath. When he turned the key in the ignition and then put the car in gear, he asked before pulling off, "You good back there?"

It took a second, but I finally responded, "Hell yeah. Thanks, baby."

I cleaned myself off and then climbed between the seats to join him up front. He looked over at me and smiled as I smiled back at him. I picked my shorts up, and as I pulled them up my legs, I told him, "I got your ass on the way back." He just shook his head, laughed, and pressed on the gas so we could proceed on our wild ride.

Chapter Nine

Mirror, Mirror on the Wall

I knew that he had been watching me. I could feel him every time I looked in my mirror. I couldn't see him, but I knew that he was there on the other side, and it turned me on. I had just moved into the apartment next door to him only two weeks ago and couldn't help but notice him on my first day. He was tall with dreads that reached the middle of his back. Dreads that I had fantasized about putting my fingers around. His eyes were a golden brown and glowed under his dark skin. His lips were full, and I had imagined them touching my skin. His legs were bowed but still, he walked with a boss swagger.

He had never spoken more than a couple of words to me but would always stare when we would pass each other. The one time I accidently brushed against him, I felt a sudden surge of pleasure. I said "excuse me" as my pussy became wet and chill bumps formed along my flesh. He was rude because he didn't even acknowledge the pleasantness in my voice. He only looked at me, nodded, and then turned away. However, his rudeness turn me on even more. It was as if he had a grudge against me, although I had never wronged him.

Every waking second of my day, thoughts of him would fill my mind. I didn't even know his name, but I wanted to say it so bad. I told myself that I had to have him, and I was determined to succeed in my mission. Tonight, I had planned on giving him a show and hoped his dick would give me a standing ovation for the performance. The mere thought of it had me moaning, "Mmm hmmm."

In my mind, he had already fucked me. I swore that I could feel his dick every time I thought of him. I imagined that it was at least nine inches long and so, so damn thick. I hoped that when it did happen—because I wouldn't stop until I did— that I would not be disappointed. However, I doubted that a man so sexy could disappoint any woman. He looked like he was packing, and I just prayed that my eyes didn't deceive me. My pussy ached just from the mere thought of it.

It had been a minute since I'd had some dick up in me, and I was due for a good fix. I needed a good fuck worse than I needed air to breathe. I had decided days ago that tonight he would get what he was looking for. I was going to perform like a professional and would make him come knocking at my door. I had it all planned out and couldn't wait to get started. Little did he know, he didn't have to keep looking through the two-way mirror, because he was more than welcome to join.

I decided to go take a hot shower and prepare myself. I hadn't thought about masturbating while I was in there, but as soon as the spray from the shower head hit my nipples, it sent a tingling message down to my pussy. I was very sexual, so it wouldn't take much to set me off and obtain an orgasm. "Oh my god. This water feels so amazing," I said out loud to myself as I put my head under it and let it flow, wetting my hair. I ran my fingers through it one good time and then to my breasts. I pushed them together, so my nipples were side by side. I then stuck my tongue out and pushed my breasts up enough for me to reach them with my mouth. I flicked my tongue over them and then pulled one into my mouth. My nipples throbbed from the suction I put on them. "Mmm hmmm," I moaned in complete pleasure as I thought about my neighbor's lips on them instead.

I finally let my breasts go and then turned to face the water. I put my right leg up on the edge and let the force of the water handle its business. I was horny and wanted to cum so bad. I grinded my hips against the flow of the water as if I had a dick already up inside of me. I spread my pussy lips and my clit popped right out like it was introducing itself for the first time to the world. I placed a finger on top of it and pressed really hard and then rotated it in a circular motion. "Oh, yes. Mmm, yeah," I called out as I let the water fuck me.

I leaned my head back and masturbated my clit faster. "Oh, yeah, I'm gonna cum." I could feel the pressure building and knew that I would be cumming really soon. "Yeah, yeah. Oh yes, mmm hmm." My clit became numb from the amount of force I had on it, which would only make the orgasm even more intense. "Oh god, I'm cumming. Yes, I'm fucking cumming," I screamed out as my juices squirted out of my pussy hole. The flow of the water washed away my dirty deed as soon as I committed it. I slowed my finger down and when I pulled it away, I put it in my pussy so I could coat it with my juices. I pulled it out and stuck it in my mouth so I could enjoy the essence of my core.

When I was done, I finished washing off and then without even drying my body, I wrapped my robe around me. It would be showtime soon, and I could feel my heart beat faster with every passing second. I hoped that my antics would pay off, because I wanted this nigga in the worst way. It would be hard for him to not speak to me after this show. I walked out of the bathroom and back to my bedroom so I could prepare to finish what I had started.

I heard a noise and it startled me, waking me from the unexpected sleep that I had fallen into. I knew it was him moving around as he prepared for the show I was about to give him. The show he really didn't expect from me. I sure hoped he liked surprises, because this bitch was going to blow his mind. I waited a little while just to make sure he was settled into position. I could always feel him, so I waited until his presence filled the vibes in my mind. I lay there and played like I was still asleep for about thirty minutes, and then decided the time had finally arrived, showtime.

When that feeling came over me, I pretended to be just waking up. I stretched my body out and caused the sheet that was over me to pull down some and expose my naked breasts. I usually slept in my T-shirt and panties, but this was a special occasion to me and I didn't want anything standing in my way. I kicked the sheet completely off of me and sat up on the end of the bed for a minute to gather myself, and then stood up. I walked over to the mirror that somehow gave him access to me and my privacy. I just stood there and admired my body for a second before I looked myself directly in the eyes. I swear that I could feel him looking back at me as I contemplated my next move.

I smiled at my reflection because I wanted him to know that I knew he was there behind that wall the mirror hung on. I then brought my hands up and put one on each breast. I licked my lips and placed my thumb and forefinger around each nipple as they stood straight out like thorns on long-stemmed red roses. I pinched and pulled them hard, and it caused my breasts to lift slightly. "Ugh, yes," I called out in pleasure. I closed my eyes but only for a brief second, and when I opened them, I made eye contact with myself again. I pushed one of my breasts up and pulled the nipple between my lips and let it go. I stuck my tongue out and licked around it slowly as I wet it with my saliva, and then I switched to the other one.

I finally stopped concentrating on my breasts and moved a hand down my stomach and then further down between my thighs. When I slid a finger between the folds of my pussy, I could feel the wetness that had already formed. I moved my finger back and forth over my engorged clit and looked into the mirror one more time. I brought the finger up from my clit and held it in front of me and motioned to the mirror for him to come to me. I was ready to let him know that I knew he had been watching me. I then turned my back to the mirror and walked back to my bed. I kneeled down on my knees on the edge of it and bent over so I could be exposed. I then brought my hand back between my thighs and slid my finger all the way through to my asshole and rubbed around it. When I pulled my finger back to my pussy hole, I pushed it inside and said out loud, as if he could hear me, "Ugh, yes. Oh my god, I need some dick so bad."

I pushed my finger in and out a few times and coated it with my wetness. When I stopped and pulled it out, I crawled on my hands and knees to the head of the bed and turned over to sit on my ass. I spread my legs as I rested my back against the headboard and then reached under my pillow where I had my dildo stashed and ready. I looked directly at the mirror again as I wrapped my hand around it, before I slid the rubber dick down my body and between my pussy lips.

I rubbed it over my clit for a few seconds before I went down further. I spoke out loud again and hoped that he could at least read my lips, "I need to cum all over that big black dick right now. I'm so fucking horny." I then pushed the tip of the dildo into me. My pussy wrapped around it like a snug jacket on a cold winter's day. I licked my lips as I pushed more of it into me and then pulled it back out a little while I moaned out loud in pleasure, "Mmm, yeah. Mmm hmmm."

I rotated my hips as I fucked myself with the handheld dick. I could feel my clit as it throbbed, so I took my fingers and jacked it like a small dick was attached to me. "Oh yes, yes. Ugh, I'm about to cum." My cum squirted out on the dick that I held inside of me and as it did, I pushed in and out faster. My heart was beating fast as I continued to jack my clit until it got numb again. When I was done cumming, I pulled the fake dick out of me and put it in my mouth, after I said, "This pussy tastes so good. You should come try a little." I then sucked and licked all of my juice off it.

When I was done, I got up off the bed and walked back over to the mirror. I looked myself right in the eyes again and said to my reflection, "I know you're there. I can feel you." I paused and put my fingers on my nipples again before I continued, "Stop watching me like a coward. Show me how brave you really are and come join me." I smiled before I turned and walked away from the mirror again. I stated, "You make a bitch feel like you scared of the pussy."

I then walked away and switched extra hard so my ass cheeks would jiggle. I picked up my robe off the chair that was beside the bed and put it around me and walked out of the bedroom. I wondered now what he was thinking or even doing after the scene he had just witnessed. I knew that he would come because there was power in pussy, and when it summoned a dick, it always showed up. I went into the kitchen to get a glass of water because my activities had me thirsty. I would have rather been drinking his cum, but my throat was dry and needed relief immediately. As soon as I put the rim of the glass to my lips and took a sip, I heard a knock at my door. It startled me and made my heart feel like it was about to leap out of my chest.

I knew who it was before I even answered. I could feel his presence as I reached for the doorknob and turned. As soon as I saw him, I felt faint because he literally took my breath away. He looked me dead in the eyes and said, "You summoned me, well here I go. What you gonna do with me now?"

That was the most he had ever spoken to me and it sent chills down my spine. I shook my head from side to side and responded, "Nah, you the one that's been checking for me, so here I go. Ain't no mirror between us now."

He smiled a sexy smile that showed off his perfectly aligned teeth, and then he licked his lips before he spoke again, "Yeah, you caught me, but a nigga couldn't help himself. But now I wanna watch without the mirror." He stepped in the door and was so close that not even air could get between us, and said in a low but deep voice, "We can go in the bedroom and watch the show together if you want."

I had to close my eyes and take a deep breath, and when I opened them back up, he was no longer in front of me. I began to wonder if I had just imagined it all, until I felt him behind me. He reached around me and pushed the door shut, and then brought his hands around my waist and untied the house robe that I had on. He grabbed the flaps on each side and pulled it open. "Ugh," I let out a grunt as his fingers traced from my neck down to my arm. Then he traced around my navel before going up to my breasts. He circled the areolas that highlighted my perky nipples as I moaned, "Mmm hmmm. That feels so good."

He touched me so lightly that it made me feel fragile. He pinched my nipples between his fingers and pulled lightly while he kissed my shoulder blade. He then reached up and pulled the robe completely off my arms and let it drop in a puddle at our feet. "Oh yes," I said as he ran a finger down my spine, and when he got to the tip of my ass crack, he slid his finger down and in and traced its length.

"I've been planning this ever since you moved in," he said to me as his finger found my asshole and pressed on it. He then moved his finger past the length of flesh between my two holes. When he got to my wetness, he whispered in my ear, "This pussy wet because of me?"

I was weakened by his touch but found the strength to answer him. "Yes. Oh god, you make me so wet. I've dreamed about you doing this for a minute now. Please don't stop." I felt the tip of his finger enter me and when he pushed it further, I felt my knees buckle. "Oh my god. Yes," I cried out. He moved his finger in and out of me as I reached my hands up and behind his neck so I could hold on to him. He suddenly stopped and pulled his finger out, catching me off guard. I let his neck go and brought my arms down as I turned around and faced him.

I undid the buttons on his shirt and revealed his beautifully sculpted chest. I leaned forward and sucked one of his man nipples in between my lips. It was small but fit perfect upon his chest. He ran his fingers through my hair and then gripped a fist full and pulled my head back so I could look up at him. "I'm gonna fuck you so hard the mirror is going to feel it and shatter," he said before he moaned as I pushed his shirt back and over his broad shoulders and then down his arms. He pulled my tongue into his mouth and sucked so hard I thought he would pull it out. I reached my hands to his pants and undid them.

When he let my tongue go, I squatted down until I was right in front of his dick. It was as long and thick as I had imagined. The skin on it was dark and smooth as silk from the pressure of his hardness. The pre-cum had already formed, and I stuck my tongue out so I could lick it off. I then wrapped my lips around the head of it as he moaned in pleasure, "Mmm hmmm. Damn, that feels good." He put his hand on the top of my head as I sucked his roundness. I reached my free hand up and pulled lightly on his balls. "Yeah. That shit feels good," he told me as I sucked in another inch of him. When I started to speed up, he pulled back, stopping me, and said, "I don't wanna cum like this. Come on and let me get up in that pussy."

I smiled as I looked up at him and said, "Well, let's go. She's been waiting on you to say that." He helped pull me up from my squatting position, and then I grabbed his hand and led him to my bedroom.

When we got to my bed, I turned around and faced him. He brought his hands up to my breasts and bent his head down to pull one of my hardened nipples between his lips. He sucked lightly on it and then bit down, startling me. The sensation from his bite made me shiver, and as I moaned in pleasure, he did the same thing to the other one. "Mmm, yes. That feels good. Mmm hmmm."

He then licked his way up to my mouth and licked my lips before he said, "I wanna taste that pussy now." As soon as he said it, I sat down on the bed and pushed myself back a little before I laid all the way down. I spread my legs for him as he crawled up to me and rested his elbows between my thighs. It had been so long since a man's mouth had been in my garden, and I was so wet and ready for him to take me to another world.

He spread my pussy lips with his soft fingers and as soon as my swollen clit popped out, he sucked it into his warm mouth. "Oh my god, yes," I cried out as he sucked it hard but slow. He flicked his tongue over my womanhood as he sucked, giving me extra pleasure. "Mmm, oh god. You gonna make me cum so hard. Yes. Please don't stop. It feels so damn good." I put my hand on top of his head and gripped his dreads between my fingers so I could hold him hostage. "Mmm hmmm. Don't stop," I moaned as I pushed my pussy into his face.

I suddenly felt myself getting dizzy and knew that I had reached my limit. I moaned and cried out, "Mmm, yes, I'm about to cum. Yes. I'm cumming." No sooner than I said it, my cum squirted out and on to his chin. He continued to suck on my clit as I came, and the feeling was so intense that I let go of his dreads and gripped the sheets. I tried to pull up from him because he was making me crazy, but he wrapped his arms around my thighs and gripped them so tight I couldn't move in any direction. I continued to cry out, "Oh my god. Oh, oh god. Oh, ugh, please, please." When I was done cumming, he finally released my legs, and I lay there dazed and breathing heavily. He got up and repositioned himself on his knees, now with his dick in his hand.

He asked, "You sure you ready for this?"

His smile melted me as I looked at him and said, "I've never been more ready. Please give me that dick. Oh my god, I want it in me so bad."

As soon as the words left my mouth, he put the head of his dick at my pussy hole. He gripped my knees and pushed my legs up to my breasts, and then he pushed his length into me slowly, inch by inch. "Damn, this pussy is tight," he said as he looked at me and smiled. He then added, "Don't worry, though, I'm about to loosen this bitch up." He pulled out and then pushed back into me harder and asked, "How you want me to give this dick to you?"

I looked him in the eyes and winked as I put my fingers around my nipples and played with them, and then I answered him, "I want that dick to beat this pussy up. Make this little bitch sore. She's long overdue." He pulled out again and slammed into me harder. "Ugh, shit," I blurted out from the force of him, and then said, "You acting like you scared to fuck this pussy. Nigga, put that dick to work."

He pulled out again and then pulled my legs back to straighten them out. He placed them over his shoulders and then pushed them down to my chest as far as they would go, and said to me, "Alright. But remember, you asked for this."

He went all the way into me hard and rotated his hips as he did. I swear I could feel him deep in my chest as he hit my walls with no mercy at all. I cried out in pleasure, "Yes, oh yes. Nigga, fuck this pussy harder. Fuck me, yes." I looked over and into the mirror as he pounded into me and watched as his ass muscles clenched and then unclenched every time he pushed and pulled.

He asked me in between thrusts, "That hard enough for you? Huh? This dick fucking you like you want it to?"

"Oh my god, yes. This dick is so good. Yes. Keep fucking me hard. You feel so damn good inside of me," I screamed in pure ecstasy as he continued to pound into my pussy harder.

He then turned his head to the mirror and watched as he fucked me. He said, "This pussy about to make me cum, Shit."

I reached my hand down between my legs and masturbated my clit because I wanted us to cum together. I said, "Go ahead. I'm about to cum too, yeah. I'm fucking cumming. Yes, yes." About that time, I forgot all about him cumming with me as my pussy juice squirted out and completely covered his dick. He looked down at his dick, and when he saw my cum glistening on it, he slowed down a little. "What are you doing? You haven't got yours yet," I asked, because it seemed as if he was stopping.

He responded slyly, "Come on, let's get in front of the mirror. I want you to swallow it while I watch." He pulled out of me and got off the bed and stood in front of the mirror. I followed suit behind him and kneeled down in front of him while my reflection stared out at me. I then pulled him into my mouth. The flavor of my cum filled my taste buds with its essence as I deep throated him. "Yes, that feels good. Make this dick cum." He turned his focus to the mirror and watched me as I sucked him into an orgasm. "That's it. Mmm hmmm, I'm cumming right now. Shit. Swallow it. Mmm," he yelled out as his seeds shot out and went down my throat. I didn't stop sucking until he was drained of his pressure. "Damn, that shit was good," he said when I finally released his dick from the suction of my cheeks.

I looked up at him and asked, "Do you think we can still share the mirror?"

We shared a laugh as he pulled me up off my knees. We both turned and faced the mirror, and as we looked into our reflections, we said in unison, "Mirror, mirror on the wall."

Chapter Ten

Toes Up Hands Down

He sucked my toes into his mouth so sensually I almost didn't want to open my eyes. I was too afraid that he would stop. I knew that it couldn't have been a dream because it felt too good and too real. "Oh, baby, that feels so good," I said to him as he stuck his tongue out and licked between my toes now. He was a foot man and always had been. I didn't mind, though, because I loved the way he made love to mine.

"I could suck on these all day," he stated as he passed on my heels and massaged them. My feet alone could make his dick hard and he would sometimes use them as foreplay.

I finally opened my eyes and said to him in a seductive voice, "Yes, baby, you sure can."

I could see his dick poking out against the fabric of his boxer briefs. If it grew any bigger or got any harder, I was sure it would bust right through the seams the same way it did my pussy. As he continued to rub and looked me in the eyes, he said, "Now you know you ain't gotta tell me twice, ma. A nigga loves to have those feet wrapped around him." He got up and pulled his boxer briefs off, and when he got back on the bed, he repositioned himself differently. He sat at my feet and straddled them as he stretched his legs out completely straight.

His dick stood straight out with the eye of it looking at me. The pre-cum had formed, and it told me that he was ready for my touch. I took my right foot and ran my big toe over the head of his dick. His pre-cum was wet and slippery as I rubbed it over the head and into his skin. "Damn, that feels so good," he said as he enjoyed my touch.

I took my other foot and put it on his balls and kneaded them like dough, and asked him, "Do you want me to make you cum all over these feet, baby?"

He responded quickly, "Yes. Make it cum all over them for me. You know a nigga likes that shit."

"Yes, baby, I do," I said as I placed both of my feet around his dick, one on each side, and then asked him "Like that? Is this what you want? Is this gonna make that dick cum for me?"

He replied in deep frustration, "Yeah, ma, quit playing. You know what I need you to do." I pressed the bottoms of my feet a little harder against his manhood and then went up and down. Just the thought of my feet upon him brought him an immense feeling of pleasure. He was freaky like that and I loved it. "Oh, sit. Yes, baby. Go ahead and make that dick cum," he cried out as I jacked his dick with my feet as fast as they would go.

"Cum for me, baby, come on, cum on these feet for me," I said as I kept a steady pace.

He leaned back on his hands and enjoyed the feeling I gave to him. I knew it wouldn't take him long because it never did when my feet touched him. "Yeah, baby, don't stop, you about to make me cum," he said, and not even thirty seconds later, his cum shot out and all over my feet. "Yeah. Shit. Yes, baby, Oh," he cried out in pleasure as I rubbed his cum all over his dick with the bottoms of my feet.

After he was done cumming, I got up and crawled down to him. I rested my elbows on the bed in between his thighs. His dick had softened a little from the orgasm he had just received, but I refused to let it go completely down. I grabbed his length and ran my tongue down it and licked his juices off of it. "Mmm," I moaned in response, because I was not about to let his dick go until it was just the way I liked it. Long, fat, and really, really hard.

I could feel my pussy as it throbbed really hard and waited patiently for some dick, but her turn would come soon enough. He reached a hand up and placed it on the back of my head and stated, "Damn, you can make a dick feel good. That shit feels so damn wonderful."

As he talked to me, I sucked hard and moaned, "Mmm hmmm." I put a hand under his nut sack and massaged the round orbs.

"Yeah, baby, just like that," he said as he leaned his head back in pleasure. I loved to suck his dick and would do it for hours if that's what it took. He moved his hand from my head and placed it back beside him, palm down, on the bed. As I sucked him, he pushed his hips up and fucked my mouth. I liked that rough shit, so the harder he pushed himself into my mouth, the more it turned me on. "Let me get in that pussy, baby," he said to me in between thrusts.

My pussy was wet and ready for him to beat it up, so I let his dick fall from my mouth and looked up at him. I then asked, "Are you gonna fuck it real good for me?"

I stuck my tongue out and licked around his navel and then down to his thigh, as he answered me, "Now you know I'm gonna fuck that pussy up."

I continued to lick on down his leg and then stated, "Mmm hmmm. I know that's what you better do." I had my body completely turned around now as my ass faced him. He was still leaned back on his hands, so I dropped a foot over each side of him and pushed my body back.

I grinded my ass on his dick, and as he reached a hand up and ran it down my ass crack, he asked, "Why you teasing a nigga like that?" He pushed a finger into my wet pussy and said, "Sit that pussy down on this dick and show your nigga how you want him to fuck it."

I smiled and said in response, "Move that finger then, boo. I'm trying to do bigger and better things."

He pulled his finger out and put it right in his mouth. He then put the hand around his dick and rubbed it against my wet pussy. When he put the head of it to my hole, I pushed back slowly, and when it entered me, I moved back and forth for a minute, pleasuring only the tip. "Come on, baby. Take all of this dick," he said greedily as he tried to push up so more of it could go inside of me. However, every time he pushed, I pulled back.

"Uh, uh, I'm controlling that dick today," I said to him as I continued to ride only the head. He reached a hand up and played with my asshole. He circled the roundness of it a couple of times before he finally slid his finger into me. "Oh, shit," I cried out as he violated me. "Yes, baby, oh yes. That feels so good, mmm," I said as I made all of him disappear inside of me. I rotated my hips as his length filled my walls.

"Come on, baby. Fuck this dick," he said as he pulled his finger out of my asshole and then slapped me on my ass cheek. The stinging sensation lingered for several minutes afterward.

"Yes, yes, oh baby, this dick feels so good," I cried out as I rode him backward.

He pushed up in me hard and met me thrust for thrust. "Ride that dick, ma. That pussy feels so damn good," he said as the sweat began to form on my forehead.

I rode him for only a couple more minutes, and then came off of him and said, "I want that dick up in my ass."

He made no comment as he got up and stood on the side of the bed. When he was completely in position, he demanded, "Bring that ass to me."

I turned my ass to him with my head holding me up on the mattress and then reached my hands back to spread my cheeks. He put the head of his dick to my tight hole and slowly pushed it in to me. "Uh, shit, oh my god, yes. Fuck me, baby," I cried out in pleasure as he slowly went in and out of me.

His width made me feel like he had split me wide open, but I loved it. That little bit of pain mixed with pleasure took me to a higher level of ecstasy. "You like that, ma? Huh? You like how this dick feels up in that ass?"

"Yes. Oh god, yes. Fuck me. Fuck this ass harder. Yes."

He slammed into me so hard I thought I would lose my breath. I could no longer hold my ass cheeks apart, so I let them go and brought my hands up over my head so I could grip the sheets. I pushed my face into the bed and stifled my moans. As he pounded into me, he said, "I'm...gonna...cum, ma. Yeah...shit. I'm gonna...cum."

He thrust into me a couple more times and then pulled out. I felt his wetness coat my ass cheeks, and then he rubbed it into my skin with his dick. The ceiling fan above us caused a slight chill to come over me, and the chill bumps began to pop out all over. I finally brought my head up and said to him, "Damn, that was good."

When he was done smearing his cum all on me, he turned around and went into the bathroom so he could wash his dick off. We were far from done and would only need a minute to recuperate before we would go at it again. I figured it would be a good time to make us a quick bite to eat. I got up from the bed and walked into the bathroom where he was. I wrapped my arms around him and pulled the washcloth from his grasp. I washed his dick, lightly covered it with suds, and said, "I'm gonna go prepare us a little something to eat because you need all that nutrition you can get before I drain you." He laughed and turned his head to the side to kiss me. I kissed him back and let go of the washcloth, leaving it hang up on his dick.

I walked into the kitchen and decided to cook us a breakfast meal because I knew it was his favorite, and I always tried to please him. As the aroma of eggs and bacon filled the kitchen, I heard him walk up behind me and say, "Smells good. But not as good as that pussy." I laughed as he put his arms around me in a romantic gesture. My nipples reacted to his touch as they always did, and I knew right then that I would be feeding him more than breakfast. He said, "I want that pussy on a plate, not some bacon and eggs."

I slapped his hand away and turned the stove off and said, "Come on, baby. I need you to be fully energized for this pussy, 'cause it still needs a lot of work done on it."

He held his hands up like he was being arrested and backed away. He said, as he turned and went to the table, "Okay. Okay, but your ass is gonna pay for making me wait." He pulled his chair out and sat down so I could bring him his food. I put his plate in front of him and then sat down in the opposite chair as he licked his lips. I put a piece of bacon in my mouth and pulled it out slowly as he ate his meal. I smiled at him and shrugged my shoulders and decided to give him a little bit of pleasure. "Thank you, baby. This is really good," he said to me politely and continued to eat.

I lifted my leg under the table and stretched it across, resting it on his knee. He looked at me and lifted an eyebrow and asked, "What you think you doing under there?" I sucked another piece of bacon through my lips instead of answering him. I then ran my toes along his inner thigh and found his dick hanging low. He had on his robe, but because of the way he was sitting, it had opened up just enough to give me access. I lifted his dick with my foot and balanced it on the top of it. He ate his food and acted as if what I was doing didn't affect him, but I knew better. He was just playing hard. I let his dick fall back between his legs and ran the bottom of my foot over it until I felt it start to grow. "Ma, you fucking me up right now," he said as he licked his lips and smiled at me.

I moved my foot and pushed my chair back and said to him, "Don't mind me, baby. Just keep eating your food." I then scooted out of my chair and disappeared under the table. I crawled to him and inched myself in between his thighs. I hollered up to him, "Don't mind me, just keep eating." I had to say it a second time because I just knew that he hadn't listened. I stuck my tongue out and licked from the head of his dick to the bottom of it and back.

I licked over his balls before I sucked one into my mouth. "Shit," I heard him blurt out as I sucked nice and slow. I then heard his fork fall to the table, making a clattering sound, and suddenly, his hands appeared underneath. He didn't push his chair back or anything, but instead, he placed both of his hands on my head and said to me, "Suck it for me, ma. Make a nigga get right."

I let his balls go and lifted them so I could get to his asshole. I licked the wrinkles around it and slowly jacked his dick at the same time. He scooted in the chair until his ass was on the edge and leaned back, and I slid my finger into him and moaned, "Mmm."

He flinched at the violation and asked, "Why you always catch me off guard with that shit?" I pulled his dick to my mouth and wrapped my lips around it so I could give him double the pleasure. "Yeah, ma, yeah, do that shit right there." Since I had his dick locked down in my mouth and he couldn't move, he pushed the table back instead, so he could get to me. I cut my eyes up at him once he did that. He utilized the front of his robe and let it fall completely open. It draped around the legs of his chair like a curtain, as he said, "Get up so I can get in that pussy again."

I let his dick go and came up off my knees to stand. He put his arms under my arm pits and helped lift me. He then pushed everything off the tabletop and lifted me, planting my ass on the table's edge. He grabbed my legs and wasted no time spreading them. I leaned back on my hands as he positioned himself at my opening, and then he leaned forward to pull me into a kiss.

After he kissed me, I laid all the way back on the table. He wasted no time as he pushed his dick into me with a vengeance and caused me to gasp. "Ugh." He then pulled one of my feet up and sucked on my toes as he plunged in and out of me. "Yes, baby, you feel so good," I cried out as I brought my hands to my breasts so I could play with my nipples.

I twisted and pulled on them until they became numb, and then I moved one of my hands down to my clit as he said to me, "Make that little motherfucker feel good, baby." I did as he said and pressed on my clit before I started to jack it, and he continued going in and out of me. "Yeah, I'm about to fill this pussy up," he said as he grabbed both of my ankles and held my legs straight up.

"Mmm, yes. Fuck me, baby. Fuck me good," I yelled and moaned as I continued to pleasure my clit. I felt him suddenly slow down as his dick pulsed inside of me. I knew that he was about to coat my walls with his essence, and I was so ready for it. He slammed into me one last time, and as his body shook, he shot his seeds inside of me. "Oh, baby, I'm cumming too," I cried out to him as we came in sync.

He pulled out of me really slow after we both were done, and then bent down, putting his head between my legs. He made a trail of kisses up to my stomach and then on up to my breasts before he pulled a nipple into his mouth. I ran my fingers over his hair and moaned in pleasure, "Mmm hmm," as he sucked on my nipple hard. He let it go and did the same thing to the other one before coming up and kissing me. He then traced his tongue down my body until he got to my throbbing clit. I flinched as he pulled the hood back and flicked his tongue over it, and I said, "No, baby, she's still sensitive. I don't think I can handle it right now."

I then tried to pull myself up, but he took my legs and placed them to where my thighs were over his shoulders. He grabbed my wrists and locked his hands around them so I couldn't move. He pulled my clit back into his mouth and sucked on it hard as he flicked his tongue over it. I screamed, as I tried to get away from him, "Oh my god. No, baby, no. Shit, oh, oh baby, oh." He enjoyed what he was doing even more because he knew that he was torturing me. My clit was still so sensitive from when I had been masturbating it. It throbbed harder the longer he sucked, and I could feel another orgasm building. "Oh shit, shit, shit, shit. Baby, you about to make me cum again. Shit," I cried out in ecstasy right before the flood gates opened.

I gripped his head really hard as my cum squirted out into his goatee, the orgasm weakening me. He let my clit go and pushed his tongue into my open pussy so he could quench his thirst. I laid there and breathed heavily because, well, I just couldn't do anything else. He knew just how to put me in my place, and I enjoyed every second of it. He finally came up for air and let my legs and wrists go free, and then pulled me up to him and asked, "You okay, ma? Damn, a nigga got you like that."

His smile melted me, as always, and I somehow found the strength to respond to him, "Yeah, baby. That shit was good. But you know I'm gonna get your ass back for that one."

I tiptoed and wrapped my arms around his neck, pulling him into another kiss. He lifted me, and as I wrapped my legs around his waist, he put his hands under my ass to keep me balanced. He said, "Don't worry, you can get me back right now." He turned toward the bedroom and carried me right back to where it all started.

I knew that I was in for a long night and was ready. His stomach was full, his dick was heavy, and his mouth was always ready and waiting for me to put my toes in it. When we got to the bedroom, he laid me on the bed gently and then dropped his robe to the floor. After he did, he started to get on the bed, but I put a foot against his chest to stop him. He looked down at me and smiled before he reached his hands up and grabbed my foot. When he did, I pulled it back and said, "Uh, uh, I want it on that dick, baby. Remember, toes up, hands down."

Chapter Eleven

Home Alone and Horny

I laid there and rotated my hips against his face as his tongue found my asshole and swirled around it, and he sucked its edges at the same time. He had his finger deep inside my pussy, using the come here motion as his thumb pressed on my clit, driving me literally insane. Only he had the power to make me cum back to back. I had many lovers in my day, but none that were as skilled as the one who had been between my thighs all night. No matter how hungry I was, he could always curb my sexual appetite.

His Caesar was cut to perfection, edged on a face that should have been on the cover of *People* magazine, because he truly was the sexiest man alive. "Oh, baby, yes. You gonna make me cum again," I just fully cried out to him as he hit my G-spot and made my insides tremble. With his finger still inside of my pussy, he pushed another one into my asshole. "Oh, shit. Yes, that feels so good," I screamed out as he doubled the pressure. I rotated my hips a little faster so that I could match his rhythm, and as soon as he pulled my engorged clit between his lips, I went crazy. "Oh. Oh, yes. Oh my god, yes. I'm gonna cum, yes, yes. I'm gonna cum."

No sooner than I said it, my walls erupted and my cum squirted all over his finger. "Yes, baby, that's it," he stated as I tightened my ass muscles. "Mmm hmmm. That's what I like. Give me all of it," he said right before he pulled his finger out of me and replaced it with his tongue, and then he looked up at me and asked, "You wanna take a shower with me?"

I turned my eyes to him and stated, "You're not gonna finish what you started?"

He knew that I wanted some dick, but from the sound of it, he wasn't going to give any of it up. He thumped my clit really hard with his fingers as it continued to throb from the orgasm he had given me only minutes before, and said, "I can't be late today. Sorry, but you know that when I stick my dick in all that good pussy, I don't want to come out." He rose from the bed, and as I watched his muscles lift him, I became a little upset. As his dick swung between his thighs, he said, "Don't worry, I'll make it up to you later."

I sat up and leaned against the headboard and spread my legs. He stopped in his tracks when I pushed one of my small fingers into my pussy and said greedily, "Sure you don't want to reconsider?"

He shook his head from side to side as he stood there for a minute, lost in thought. He then walked up to the side of the bed and leaned over. I thought that he was giving in to my persuasions, but he just kissed my forehead instead and said, "Nah, baby. I got an important client coming for this meeting. I'm the CEO and I can't be late." He stood back up, and before he walked into the bathroom, he turned back around and said, "I promise, I'm gonna make it worth the wait." He winked at me and then smiled that sexy smile that I loves so much, and then turned around and disappeared from my view.

I lay there and pouted for a minute before I gave up trying to get fucked. I knew he meant what he said and decided that when he left for work, I would take care of my own needs one good time just to hold me over until he got back. I went ahead and got up so I could join him in the shower. When I walked in, he was washing his dick and nut sack, so I walked up to the shower and asked, "Do you need some help with that heavy load?"

He laughed and handed me the soapy washcloth and said, "Yeah, some extra muscle might be okay. But don't come in here fucking around. You know I gotta get ready and get to work." I laughed, and with the soapy cloth in my hand, I stepped into the shower with him.

I lifted his long dick and washed it softly. I made sure to get the edges of the head of it and then on down to the base and under. He watched me the entire time but said nothing as I did my thing. I lifted his dick so I could get to his nut sack, and as I washed under it, I heard a moan escape his lips. "Mmm, shit." I looked up at him and saw that he had leaned his head back and now had his eyes closed. I took advantage of the situation and pushed the washcloth all the way through his legs so I could get to his ass. I washed between the crack slowly and sensually and paid extra close attention to his asshole.

I washed his hole thoroughly and then let the washcloth fall from my grasp. When it hit the shower floor, it startled him, and he looked down to see what had happened, but I didn't care and didn't bother to stop what I was doing. His ass crack was slippery because of the soap suds, so I took advantage of it and let my finger slide right into him. "Shit, baby, come on. You gonna make a nigga late for they job. Mmm, mmm, shit," he stated matter of factly as I violated his inner core.

I asked, as I looked up at him with innocence in my eyes, "Do you want me to stop? Because I will." I knew that once I had my finger going good, he would let me continue.

"No, no. Damn, that feels good. I gotta hurry, though. Shit," he said as he began to thrust against my hand.

I moved a little and let the water run over his dick so it would wash the suds away and I could suck it. I said, right before I pulled him between my lips, "Don't worry, I'm about to make you cum really quick," and he knew that I would keep my word.

Once the suds were gone, I removed my finger from his ass but only long enough to bring my hand back a little and grasp his balls with the palm of my hand. Once they were securely in my palm, I pushed back enough to push my finger back inside of him. I figured that I'd be killing two birds with one stone that way. I used my other hand to lift his most prized possession, and then I sucked it into my warm, wet mouth. "Slurp, slurp, mmm," I moaned as I slobbed on his dick and worked my finger in and out of him at the same time.

I could hear him above talking shit, "Suck it, baby. You wanted this motherfuckin' anaconda, so suck that shit like you mean it. Yeah. Just like that." My cheeks sunk in as I sucked with all my might. I knew that I was good at what I did, and it didn't take much longer to pump his well dry. I kneaded his balls and fucked his asshole as I thought about his cum going down my throat. I then heard him yell out in pleasure, "Yeah, baby, I'm cumming. Swallow it. Swallow all of it, yes, yes, baby. Yes."

He grabbed a hold of my head so he could steady himself and pumped into my mouth one last time really hard. His ass muscles tightened as his cum shot out and flowed like a river down my throat. I had refused to let him go until every single drop came out of him. I then pulled my finger out but continued to knead his balls for a few more seconds. I let them go when I heard him say, "Damn, baby, a nigga needed that release. I'm gonna reward you really good when I get back, so have that pussy ready."

I let his balls go and stood up to face him, and said, "Now you know this pussy stays ready for you."

He kissed me on the lips and got out of the shower while I stayed in and took a shower of my own. Before he left, he came back in the bathroom. I was getting out of the shower when he kissed my cheek and said, "You might as well stay naked until I get back. That way, I can dive right in," and then he laughed and walked out.

His sense of humor was what had attracted me to him in the first place. Other men had only made me smile, but he made me smile and laugh from deep within. He found things funny when others wouldn't have, and his laugh was infectious, keeping me laughing with him. I knew that I was about to have a long day and would think about him as the hours ticked away. I grabbed a T-shirt and threw it over me but nothing else. I was going to sit in front of the television while he was gone, so I got a drink and some snacks out of the kitchen and perched myself on the plush leather couch.

I flipped through the channels but found nothing interesting to watch, so I decided to put in a DVD. When I got up to put the disc in, the T-shirt I had on slid between my ass cheeks, and when I pulled it out, it gave me a chill that reached to my clit and made it pulse. I laughed to myself and continued with the task at hand. I put in a porn movie that we had purchased but hadn't had a chance to watch yet. My man had left me hanging, so I figured I'd watch the next bitch get hers instead.

I watched as the screen filled with the image of a woman lying in bed. The covers only concealed her bottom half. Her breasts were splayed out on her chest like mini-mountains waiting to be climbed. "Hmmm, nice," I said to the television, as if the woman I had in view could hear me. The areolas around her fat nipples were dark brown in color and accented the caramel color of her skin. She woke up and looked around the room she was in, and then turned her eyes in my direction. It was as if she could see me looking at her. She spoke to the screen, but I knew her words were meant for me. "Oh gosh, I'm so horny right now," she said, and then she licked her lips as I watched and anticipated her next move.

She wrapped her fingers around her nipples and rubbed them while she moaned in pleasure, "Mmm, this feels really good." She then lifted her legs, allowing the covers to fall off of them. She looked at me again and said, "I sure wish I had some help. I could use a nice orgasm." She lifted one of her breasts up and stuck her tongue out of her mouth. It was long and fat, and the tip of it was pointed. I could see her saliva glistening in the light as she put the tip of it on her nipple and licked over it. She stopped for a second. Just enough to ask, "Do you want to play in this fat pussy with me?"

She flicked her tongue over her nipple right before she sucked it between her lips. She pulled on the nipple so hard I thought she would pull it off. "Mmm hmm, mmm," she steadily moaned as I felt my pussy moisten. The screen then went between her thighs and showed her shaved pussy. Her clit was fat and was protruding between her pussy lips, looking as if it was about to burst. I could see wetness at the opening of her inner core, and the feeling it gave me caused me to flinch. She then said seductively, "Come on and watch me make this pussy cum. She's gonna squirt all over your wildest imagination. Mmm hmmm."

She traced a finger from her breast to her pussy and rubbed on the part of the clit that was poking out, and asked, "This pussy is fat, ain't it?" She giggled to herself and continued, "Do you like fat pussy? Do you want to watch as I make this fat pussy cum? Yeah, I know you do. Are you ready?"

I didn't know the bitch on the screen, but I liked her sex appeal. She had my pussy wet and aching, and no one was there to give me what I needed. I moaned when she spread her pussy lips apart. "Mmm. Mmm." Her creamy filling drained from her innermost part. For some reason, it made me lick my lips and want to taste it.

When she pressed her middle finger on the top of her clit and started to rotate it, my legs spread apart on their own accord. I sat up and pulled the T-shirt from over my head as my feet rested on the coffee table in front of me. The woman in the screen said, "Come on and follow my lead." I then put my finger on my clit and rotated it in small, circular motions. The pleasure caused another moan to escape my lips, "Mmm hmmm."

She spoke again, "Now doesn't that feel good? I bet your pussy is so wet right now. I wish that I could taste it as the cum flows out of you." She paused, but for only a brief second, and continued, "Go ahead and push that finger up in there. Make that pussy feel even better. Yes, yes. Just like that." She moved her middle finger down to her wet hole and pushed it inside while I followed suit and did the same. "Oh, yes. Yes, this feels so good, but I think I have something that will feel a little better," she said as she reached over and picked up a long pink dildo. She looked at me with it in her hand, and said with a smile on her pretty face, "Now this is what I'm talking about. This right here should fill me up. I sure wish you could help me get it up in there." She licked the tip of it and then said, "I know that you have one of these, because if you're looking at me right now, that means you're a freak just like me. Mmm hmmm. I know."

I paused the DVD with the remote so I could go to the bedroom and get my toy. It wasn't quite as big as the one she had in her hand, but it was close, and it would just have to do. After grabbing the substitute dick, I hurriedly went back to the couch as my breasts bounced from the movement. I sat back down and scooted my ass to the edge of the seat and placed my feet back on the table. I then said to the television, while I pushed play again, "Now I'm good and ready."

The woman on the screen put the handheld dildo into her mouth and sucked it like it was a real dick. Her saliva covered it and made it wet as she moaned, "Mmm hmmm." I sucked on the head of the one I had at the same time and enjoyed it as if it was attached to a set of balls. I imagined it belonged to my man and sucked with great precision. I closed my eyes for a second and then opened them back up so I could watch her next move.

She pulled the dildo from her mouth slowly, inch by inch, and then rubbed the head of it over her erect nipples one at a time. "Oh, yes, that feels so good," she said as she looked at me.

I continued to follow her movements as the dildo in my hand brushed over my nipples. "Yes, it does feel good," I said back to her, as if she could hear me talking to her, and in a way, I wished that she could.

She then spoke again, "I bet you're ready to push that dick up inside of you. Aren't you?" She chuckled and added, "I know my pussy is ready. It stays ready, and I bet yours does too."

I responded, "Yes, yes, it does. It is so ready."

She ran the dildo down her torso and to her navel. She circled it with the toy before she guided it down a little further. When it hit her clit, she flinched. "Oh my goodness. It's so sensitive," she stated lustfully as the dildo slid in between her pussy lips.

I felt the same sensation as the one in my hand went over my clit and between my swollen pussy lips. Together, we glided the fake dick back and forth over our clits. Both of us moaning and enjoying the pressure that was building inside. "Ooh, uh, mmm, hmmm. Yes."

We grinded our hips and pleasured our pearls simultaneously. I was ready to get fucked, but she took her time getting us to that point, making the outcome even more intense. I thought of leaving her behind and going for what I wanted all by myself. I pushed the head of the dildo closer to my wet hole, and when I placed it directly at it so that I could push it in, she spoke again, "Uh, uh. Don't be selfish and leave me behind. I want our pussies to cum together."

I was blown away because it was almost as if she could sense what I was doing. Although, I knew she really didn't know how close I was to pushing the dildo inside of me. I stopped and decided to wait until she told me when to fuck myself.

"Good girl, now, let's proceed," she said as she spread her legs wider to gain better access. I spread mine with her and held the dildo tight, as if it would try to escape my grasp, but I wasn't letting this bad boy go for nothing in the world. "Now, let's fuck this dick like there's a man attached to it," she said as the head of it slid inside of her.

I said to her, as if she could hear me, "It's about damn time." I pushed the head only into me and moaned in relief, "Mmm, yes. Finally." Together, we pushed a little more inside and continued until it was all the way to the end. If our hands hadn't been in the way, holding on, it would have gotten lost in the dark tunnel and made its own path.

"Oh, yes, yes. Oh my god, I'm gonna cum so hard," I cried out as I pushed and pulled on the toy inside of me.

"Yeah, that's it. Fuck that pussy and make it cum," she said as I sped up.

"I'm gonna cum. Oh yes, I'm gonna cum so hard. Fuck. Yes," I hollered out.

And as if she heard me, she responded, "Yes, go ahead and cum for me. Cum all over that dick. Yes, girl. I'm gonna cum with you. Fuck that pussy harder so we can cum together. Yes, that's it."

I pushed and pulled only a few more times and felt myself get dizzy. I knew that I was about to cum all over the dildo. I thought about my man and envisioned him pushing into me instead. "Yes, yes, yes," I cried out one last time as my cum covered the fake dick.

My wetness made it slippery, and as I wondered about my partner on the screen, I suddenly heard her cry out, "I'm cumming, oh yes, his pussy is cumming. Oh my god. Yes, yes." I opened my eyes and watched as her creamy wetness covered the pinkness of her handheld man. She pulled the sex toy out of her once she was done, and I followed suit. She said to me, "Now, put it in your mouth and taste what drives those men out there crazy." She sucked the dildo into her mouth and removed all of her juice from it, before she pulled it back out and said, "Mmmm, tastes so damn good, doesn't it?" She smiled at the screen and said, "I had a wonderful time, but I have to go now. Someone else needs my assistance. But please, make sure you 'cum' again. I'll be waiting for you," and then the screen went black.

"Oh my god. That was so wonderful," I said out loud to myself as I sat there for a minute, getting my strength back. I was so relaxed that I ended up falling asleep. I wasn't sure how much time had passed, but I was suddenly awakened by someone pinching my nipple. "Ow, shit," I cried out as I opened my eyes and saw my man as he stood above me.

I smiled at him as he held up the dildo that I had been too exhausted to even get up and put away. He asked, "Damn, baby, you cheating on a nigga with this?" He laughed lightly and then ran the dildo over my breasts.

I moaned and answered him, "Mmm. Baby, I thought about you the entire time."

"Oh yeah?" he said right before he started getting undressed.

"What you doing? My little friend here might get jealous," I stated, referring to the dildo.

He looked at me and said, "Nah, I'm just going to show him how a real man gets down, baby girl."

I watched as he pulled the polo shirt from over his head. Every time I saw his sculpted chest was like the first time. I thought about helping him but decided against it because I was turned on more by watching him. I decided to talk shit to him so he would get even more hyped up. "You shouldn't have left me home alone and horny. Had to get another dick up in here to do what you should have handled before you left."

As he pushed his Dickies down around his ankles and stepped out of them, he looked up at me and said, "Don't worry. I'm about to make you forget all about this little nigga here." As his balls swung behind his semi-hard dick, he said to me, "Daddy's about to put that nigga to shame."

I laughed as he talked shit about the dildo. I then looked from his eyes to his dick and got serious. I licked my lips and said, "Mmm. You already putting that nigga to shame and you ain't even put in no work yet." I reached my hand out and ran a fingernail around the lining of the head, and I watched it grow from my touch.

"Yeah, ma. That shit tickles," he said as he closed his eyes for only a brief second. When he opened them back up, he reached a hand out and pulled my nipple, lifting my breast up a little, and said, "Come on and suck it up for me, baby. Get it right so I can fuck that good ass pussy."

I looked up at him one last time as I scooted all the way to the edge of the couch and planted my feet on the floor. I sucked him all the way in and then stopped. I said, "Come on and sit down so I can do what I do best." He didn't protest as we switched places. He sat so close to the edge his balls hung off the couch. I got between his thighs as he propped his feet up on the coffee table the same way I had mine earlier. He then leaned all the way back as I went to work on him.

"Yeah, baby, that feels good. Is that the way you sucked that little nigga off earlier?" he asked as he put both of his hands on the back of my head and pushed into me.

"Mmm hmmm," I responded as I continued to suck his length. I reached my free hang up and gripped his balls as he moaned and enjoyed the feeling I was giving him.

"Mmm. Yeah, baby. Yeah, mmm, yes." I didn't want to suck his dick any longer because I was ready for it to be inside of me. I let it fall out of my mouth and pushed up so his hands could no longer hold my head down. He looked at me crazy and asked, "What the fuck you doing, ma?"

I answered him greedily, "Nigga, I want this dick in my pussy. I've been waiting on it all day." I then turned my back to him and spread my ass cheeks and said, "Got a bitch depending on a rubber dick and shit to fuck her right. You ain't getting out of this one." I backed up until his dick was right under my pussy hole and slid down. I moaned in pleasure as he disappeared inside of me. "Oh yeah, baby. Yes. Mmm, it feels so good."

He responded, "Better than that nigga from earlier?"

I smiled as he went deep, and said, "Oh yeah, baby. This dick is so much better."

I leaned over and placed my hands on top of his feet while I contracted my pussy muscles. He grabbed my ass and squeezed tightly as he asked, "Does that dick feel good to you? Huh? You ridin' the hell out of this dick, baby. You gonna make a nigga cum real quick."

His voice motivated me to go faster as sweat began to break out on my forehead, "Yeah. Cum for me. I want to cum with you. Make me cum with you," I cried out as I winded my hips and slammed into him.

He told me, "Move your hands and put them on the table so I can pull my feet down. I want to punish that pussy for not waiting on me." I did as he said one hand at a time, and once my hands were secured on the table's surface, he pulled his feet down. When he planted them on the floor, he grabbed my hips and held on to them as he lifted up from the couch. His dick never fell out of me as he pushed me so that my feet planted themselves on the floor. He said, "Nah, ma, put those knees up on that table too. I wanna go deep in that pussy."

I lifted one leg at a time onto the table in front of me, and when both were in place, I bent all the way over, leaving an arch in my back. "That's right, baby. That's just how I want it," he said as he pushed all of his length into me really hard.

As he held on to my hips and rammed into me, I cried out in complete pleasure, "Yes, baby, yes, fuck me harder. Make this pussy cum for you. Yes." I felt his open hand slap my ass cheek and flinched from the stinging sensation. The pain added to the pleasure he was already giving me. "Oh, baby. I'm gonna cum all on this dick. Yes. I'm gonna cum," I said as I reached a hand between my legs and played with my clit to intensify the orgasm. "

Oh yeah. You gonna cum on a nigga. Do it, baby. This is your dick. Cum all over this motherfucker," he said as he pumped even faster and added, "Go ahead. I'm gonna cum with you. Yeah. Go ahead, baby. Squirt that shit all over this dick." About that time, my pussy squirted its cum all over his dick. He pushed into me one final time and stopped for a brief second as his vein pulsed and his love juice covered my walls. "Ugh, ugh," he grunted as he pulled out just a little and then slammed back into me. He stopped once more, and I felt it as his knees buckled while he erupted everything into me.

When he was done, he pulled out slowly and then sat back on the couch. I got off the table and he grabbed my wrist and pulled me down on the couch beside him as we both breathed heavily. We just sat there for a few minutes, catching our breath, and then he finally broke the silence. "I bet you won't give all that good ass pussy to that rubber motherfucker again."

I laughed ran a finger over his sexy lips and said, "Hmmm, you don't ever know what will happen when you leave a horny bitch home alone." And I left it at that.

Chapter Twelve

Hidden Fantasy

I had admired her ever since the first day I laid eyes on her. She was by far the most beautiful woman I had ever seen. Her skin looked like it had been kissed personally by the sun itself. Her full, heart-shaped lips were covered in lip gloss and glistened like a diamond when she spoke. Her eyes were the color of strong liquor that knocked you out after just one glass and left you with a two-day hangover. Her long fingers were topped off by freshly manicured nails that I imagined trailing along my skin and leaving chill bumps in their wake. My mouth watered at the sight of her, and my clit pulsed hard as if it was going to break free from between my pussy lips just to get to her. She didn't know of all the lustful thoughts of her that filled my mind, but today would be when I told her.

"Will that be all, ma'am?" I asked as she placed her purchases on the counter. "Yes. Thank you. That will be it," she said as she pulled out her credit card. I rang up her items as the scent of her attacked my sense of smell and stimulated the innermost part of my adrenaline. It spiked to its highest level, and I had to close my eyes for a brief second just to regain my composure. "Ma'am, are you okay?"

Her voice broke me from my thoughts, and when I opened my eyes, I smiled at her and answered, "Yes. Oh, yes, I'm so sorry. My mind had just ventured to forbidden places." She smiled back at me and reached her smooth hand across the counter to hand me the credit card. I stared into her eyes as I reached for it.

At that moment, I was at a loss for words because her boldness outweighed mine. I hadn't yet planned my next move because I didn't expect things to go this way. I finally stood back up straight and asked, "What did you have in mind?"

She stood back up before she responded, "Here's my address. I'll be there waiting to share your visions." She handed me a piece of paper after she had written on it, and when I looked at it, I read off her address. She picked up her purchases without waiting for a response and walked to the door. Before she walked out, she turned and said, "Don't stand me up."

It felt like the rest of the day dragged along. The anticipation of being next to her was driving me insane. I had never thought that she would be down like this, but now that I knew she was, I became more nervous than ever. I would have to gain my composure before going to her place and knew just how I was going to do it. I clocked out, happy that the workday was over, and rushed home to prepare myself. As soon as I walked into my condo, I stripped off everything I had on. I went straight to my closet to find something with easy access to wear and decided on a wraparound dress that tied on the side. One pull of the belt and it would fall open. It was my favorite piece of clothing.

I went in the bathroom and ran some bath water, adding vanilla bath salt to it. I wanted to smell good enough to eat and hoped the scent would make her even hungrier. After the tub was full, I got in and laid back, enjoying the warmth of the water. "Oh, this feels so nice," I said out loud as I closed my eyes. On instinct, my hands began to explore my body. I ran my fingers over my hardened nipples and pinched them lightly, leaving a stinging sensation. I ran my other hand down between my legs so I could take care of the throbbing feeling just in case things didn't go as planned.

I flinched when my finger found my clit and on instinct, spread my legs. "Mmm," I moaned as I pressed my finger hard up against my womanhood. I did small, circular motions over the hardness until I felt myself get dizzy. "Shit. Yes. Mmm hmm," I moaned out loud in pleasure. I went faster and pressed harder until my creamy juices clouded the water. "Oh. Oh yeah, oh," I cried out as I released the pressure until it faded away. I then continued my bath and thought of all the things I was going to do to her.

I stayed in the tub longer than I expected to. I didn't want to show up at her place too early, but I didn't want to be too late either. As the clock showed the time of seven twenty, I decided it was time to get ready to fulfill my fantasy. I put on my dress after I rubbed my body down with Victoria's Secret vanilla-scented lotion and pulled my hair up into a messy ponytail. I didn't fully know what tonight would bring but couldn't wait to get there and find out.

I put her address into my GPS as soon as I started my car and let it led me to paradise. I pulled up in an affluent community and knew that she did well for herself. When I made it to the single-story stucco, I pulled in the driveway and cut my engine off. My heartrate began to speed up, so I sat there for just a minute before I got out of my car. When I finally did get the nerve, I stepped out into the night breeze. It caused my nipples to harden and poke out from under the sheer fabric. The click-clack of my heels led me to her front door, and before I even had a chance to ring the bell, the door opened.

I looked up, and when I saw her standing there, my knees became weak. She held a glass of wine in her hand as she spoke, "I almost gave up on you. Please, come in."

I pulled the screen door open and stepped into her abode and said to her, "I wouldn't have missed this for anything in the world." She closed the door behind me and offered me a glass of what she was drinking. "I'd love some," I said as I watched her hips sashay past me and to her mini bar. I followed behind her and plopped down on one of the bar stools and said, "This is a nice place you have here."

She looked up at me and smiled and said, "Thank you. Make yourself at home." After she poured my drink, she came from around the bar and sat on the stool beside me.

"Thanks," I said as I took the glass from her hand and sipped slowly. The refreshing liquid glided down my throat and quenched my thirst.

After I sat my glass down, she asked, "So, what have you thought about when you look at me?"

The question caught me off guard, and I was not prepared to answer it. "Uhm, well…" I started to say, but she stopped me.

"It's okay, you really don't have to answer. I'd rather you show me instead." She stood up from her seat and opened the silk robe that she had on and dropped it to the floor. She said, "You don't have to fantasize and wonder anymore. I can make all your visions become reality."

She reached a hand up the slit of my dress and caressed my thigh, and as she leaned over to kiss me, I inhaled a deep, much-needed breath. Her lips were soft and tasted like watermelon. "Mmm," I moaned as she sucked my tongue in to her mouth. She sucked it hard, and I hoped that she would suck on my clit with the same intensity. As she reached a hand to the belt on my dress, she never broke the kiss. Once my dress was untied, she reached up and pushed it from over my shoulders. She then stopped attacking my mouth and pulled away from me.

"Come on, let's get somewhere more comfortable," she said as she reached out her hand. I put my hand in hers and got up, allowing my dress to fall completely off me and into a heap on the carpeted floor. I started to bend to pick it up, and she said, "Leave it. You won't be needing it anyway."

I stood back up straight and continued to follow her lead. Her bedroom was huge with a queen-size bed under a lone window. The decorative comforter complemented her and made the room even more inviting and appealing. "This beautiful," I said as she let go of my hand and pulled off her robe.

Her ass was as smooth as a baby's and well rounded. Not a drop of cellulite anywhere on its surface. Her spine was perfectly arched and her back was blemish free. She turned and faced me before she sat on the edge of the bed, and said, "I've been watching you too, so to find out the feelings were mutual was a wonderful surprise."

I looked from her lips to her breasts and licked my lips, before I said, "I never had enough nerve to tell you what I fantasized about. So, I would just watch you instead."

She smiled and brought a hand up to her nipple and rubbed it over it, and said, "Come over here and show me what's been on your mind."

Her erect nipples poked out like little thorns on the cacti plant. The brownness around them caused them to light up the room. She lifted one to her mouth and stuck her tongue out to lick its core. She cut her eyes up at me and said, "You gonna make me do this to myself, or you gonna come handle it?" I had never been so nervous then. I walked over to her and sat on the bed beside her. I reached up and put my hand over hers and stuck my tongue out. She moaned as both of our tongues meshed and gave her mounds the pleasure they sought. "Mmm, yes. That feels good." As I sucked on her nipples, she reached over and twisted mine between her fingers. She then said, "Hold on, let me stand."

When her breast fell from my grasp, she stood up and faced me. She then placed her foot up on the edge of the bed beside me and pulled her pussy lips apart. I reached up to touch it, but she stopped me and said, "Wait. I want you to lay back and spread your legs. Play with yours while I play with mine." She paused and then added, "Don't cum, though, I want my mouth on it when that happens." I did as she said and lay back. I pulled my legs up and spread them apart, and when I did, my pearl popped out from the folds of my pussy.

"Yes. I can't wait to suck on that one," she said as she pulled the hood back from over her fat clit. The darkness of her skin made it seem brighter than the light pink color that it was. Her actions caused me to react, and I touched my clit with a softness I had never used, before she licked one of her fingers and then put it on her clit. As she rotated her hips, I watched in anticipation. "Mmm, yes," she moaned while she leaned her head back.

I refused to lay there and do nothing. I could play with my clit at another time, it was hers I wanted to play with now. I sat up and positioned my face right in front of her pussy and said, "Let me take over now."

She looked down at me and then moved her finger and said, "Enjoy." I stuck my tongue out and flicked it over the pink flesh before I sucked into my mouth. It tasted sweet and fruity, as if it had been grown with peaches and had contracted their flavor. "Oh, yes, that feels good. Mmm hmmm, yes," she moaned as I sucked on it hard and fast. I reached a hand up and pushed two fingers into her dripping hole. The wetness covered my fingers like syrup being poured on a stack of pancakes. She placed her hand on my head and pushed her pussy to meet my thrusts. "Oh yes, suck it harder. Make me cum. Mmm," she said lustfully, and who was I to not do what she said?

"Hold on, let me lay down before I fall," she said as she giggled. I pulled my fingers out of her and let her clit pop out of my mouth, the sound echoing in the quiet of the room. She crawled on the bed and lay down and then pulled me down beside her. "Let's do the sixty-nine," she said to me as she twisted my nipple in between her fingers.

"Hey, I'm down for whatever. I just want to make you cum. You taste so good in my mouth," I stated as I turned and straddled her shoulders. I wrapped my arms around her toned thighs and dove back in.

"Mmm. Hmmm," she moaned as she pushed her tongue into my wet hole. It almost felt like a small dick was inside of me because of the way she worked it.

"Oh god, yes, I like that," I said as I let her clit go and then licked down the split of her pussy until I got to her hole. I used both hands to spread it open and licked around it. Her wetness on my tongue made me go crazy and drove me quicker to an orgasm. "I'm gonna cum. I'm gonna cum right now. Oh yes, I'm cumming," I cried out as I felt her fingers press on my clit. My cum squirted out and onto her tongue as she moaned and continued to penetrate my core. "Mmm hmmm. Mmm hmm."

The orgasm was so intense that it weakened me a little. It had been so long that it didn't take much. I was a little embarrassed, but she wasn't sweating it. She said, "Lay down. I got this."

I brought my legs from over her and lay down as she got up and straddled me. She reached under her pillow and pulled out a silver bullet and turned it on. The sounds of the vibrations filled the air as she placed her pussy on top of mine. Our clits touched, and as she began to grind against me, she stuck the bullet in between them. I was already sensitive from my orgasm, so it made me insane. "Oh my god. Oh god. Oh shit. Oh, oh, yes. Oh my god, you gonna make me cum again," I yelled out, thankful that her neighbors weren't close enough to hear me.

As the bullet vibrated between us, she gyrated her hips against me. "Mmm, yes. That feels so good, doesn't it? Yes.

Mmm hmmm," she moaned and worked the bullet back and forth. I had to grab a hold of the headboard when I felt another orgasm coming on. No man had ever made me cum back to back this way, and I enjoyed every second of it. "I'm about to cum all over your pussy," she said as she went faster. Suddenly, I felt something wet cover me and knew that she had come. "Oh yes. Yes, mmm, yes."

As she continued to work the bullet, I felt myself cumming again. "I'm cumming too. Shit," I screamed out as I let the headboard go and gripped the sheets. The second orgasm was even more intense than the first.

After we both came, she got up and lay down beside me. We were both breathing heavy but knew that we were not done. I had fantasized about her for too long to settle for that small session. No, I wanted more, and as soon as she caught her breath, I wasn't going to fuck her with the same bullet she had just used between us. I had brought my own toy and I was going to use it to return the favor. I started to get up, and she asked, "What are you doing?"

I looked at her and said, "You told me to show you my fantasy, so that's what I'm about to do."

I left her room and went back in the living room where I had left my purse and pulled out my strap-on. I turned around and saw that she had followed me. "Hmmm. Nice, much nicer than that little bullet I have," she said as she walked up to me and grabbed the strap-on from my grasp. She then bent down and placed it around me. She stood back up and sucked one of my nipples into her mouth and began to jack the strap-on at the same time. She stroked its eight inches like it was a real dick, and the pressure of it caused my clit to react. She let my nipple go and then dropped to her knees and pulled the length between her lips. Every time she went up and down it, she moaned.

I put my hand on her head and then said, "I want to put this inside of you."

She stopped sucking and looked up at me and asked, "Did you fantasize about how good it would feel inside of me?" She had turned me on from the moment I first saw her, so I had imagined ways to bring her pleasure. I wanted her time to be worth it.

"Come on, I'm ready," she said as she walked over to the couch and bent over. Her ass cheeks spread open and revealed the wetness that had been left behind from earlier. I walked up behind her and before doing anything else, I stuck my tongue out and licked from her pussy to the top of her ass crack. "Mmm, yeah," she moaned as I gripped her hips and placed the head of the strap-on dick at her pussy hole. "Ssss, shit," she cried out as the head slowly entered her wetness. I massaged her ass cheeks as I pushed all the way into her. She felt tight as her pussy gripped the roundness of the toy.

"Yes, go ahead and fuck me like a real man," she said to me as she pushed herself back.

The strap-on was my toy of choice, and I knew how to use it just right. I asked her, "Does it feel good to you? Huh? Do you like it?"

Her ass moved in waves as I pushed into her harder. She yelled out, "Yes, I like it. Make me cum all over it. Come on." I fucked her with the strap-on so hard that her feet were lifting off the ground. I could feel the lining of it rubbing against my clit every time I pushed in to her. I knew that it would not be long before I came, and I was anxious for her to cum with me. "I'm cumming on this dick. Yeah, keep going. I'm cumming," she yelled out one final time, and then I watched as her cum covered the dick. I kept pumping until I felt my knees get weak, and then I came too.

"Ma'am. Ma'am, are you okay?" I heard the woman ask me as I snapped out of my daydream. "Ma'am, I'm trying to pay for my purchases," she said as she touched my hand and tried to hand me her credit card.

"Oh my god, I am so sorry. I must have had my mind somewhere else," I said to her, embarrassed.

She said, "Yeah, your mind was pretty far away. Wanna share your thoughts?"

I could not believe that all I just shared with her did not even happen. My panties were soaked and all I could do was stare at her. I finally took her credit card and paid for her purchases and asked. "No disrespect, but do you like silver bullets?"

I could tell that she was blushing, although no one else was listening. "Why yes, I do like silver bullets. I actually have one of my own. Maybe you should stop by one day and I can show it to you." She then winked at me and smiled before she turned around and walked out.

I didn't even think to tell her that she hadn't told me where she lived. I let the thought leave my mind, and a few minutes later, she walked back inside the store. I asked, "Did you forget something?"

She looked at me with lust in her eyes and said, "Well, I came back to give you my address, but I feel like you've been there before. Hmm. That's crazy, ain't it?"

She then placed a piece of paper onto my palm and turned around once again and left. I opened the piece of paper, and when I saw her address, I was shocked because it felt like I had really been there before, in my hidden fantasy.

Chapter Thirteen

The Right to Remain Satisfied

I had always fantasized about being fucked in the back of a police car. My hands cuffed as I am taken advantage of and told that I have the right to remain silent, although I know that I won't. The officers in their dark navy-blue uniforms would slam me against the back of the police car to search me and make sure I didn't possess any weapons or drugs.

They would be rough and would have no sympathy for me because I was a criminal and didn't deserve any. With my hands secured tightly behind my back and my head pushed down onto the trunk, their hands would be all over me. "Ugh," I grunted as the hair tie holding my bun up was ripped from the strands it was used to style.

"You have the right to remain silent…" the officer behind me stated as he and his partner continued with their search.

I felt the manly hands pull me back up, and I stood there and smiled in complete pleasure. The officer's hands cupped my breasts and slightly lifted them. "I'm sorry, ma'am, but I'm going to have to remove your top so I can ensure that you have nothing concealed," one of them said in a deep voice as I listened to my buttons pop off one by one and fall to the ground, some of them hitting the back of the car before doing so.

"Do what you need to do, Officer," I said hungrily as I waited for their next move.

His partner stepped up and pulled out the handcuff key as he stated, "I'm going to remove the cuffs now because we need to be able to pull your blouse off to do a complete search." He paused as he wrapped a finger around the middle of the cuffs and added, "As long as you don't try anything crazy, we'll be able to leave them off."

I looked at him seductively and said, "Yes, Officer, I'll act accordingly."

The officer that removed the cuffs stood close as he stuck the key in the hole to unlock them. As he uncuffed me, I stretched my fingers out and brushed them across his crotch area. I could feel his semi-hard dick and couldn't wait to be able to get it completely there. "Ma'am, please keep your hands to yourself until I instruct you differently," he said to me with a smirk on his face.

"Oh yes, that feels so much better," I stated as I rubbed my wrists.

Together, the officers pulled my blouse from my shoulders and then off my arms. Once my breasts were exposed to the open air, my nipples hurriedly stood at attention and awaited their turn to be frisked. "Hmmm, what do we have here?" the white officer asked as he poked and prodded my nipples.

The black officer responded and said, "I think we should examine them thoroughly." Each of them then pulled my nipples and twisted them between their fingers.

"Oh yes," I said, because the feeling they were giving me had me on edge. When I felt their mouths pull my nipples in, I felt my clit respond. I could feel it swell in between my pussy lips trying to break free, but it would just have to wait its turn. I tried my hardest to remain still, but the way they were licking and sucking my nipples made it hard.

I finally put a hand on the back of each of their heads and moaned in pleasure, "Mmm, oh god, yes, yes. That feels so good."

The black officer let the one he was sucking go and said, "Yo, partner, I think we need to do a complete strip search. Perhaps even a cavity search."

I looked at him and smiled at his gesture. The white officer finally let my other nipple go and turned to his partner and said, "I agree. Please step away from the car, ma'am."

I smiled and asked, "Should I call my lawyer?" Neither of them answered, but instead, they started stripping me of the rest of my attire. Once they had me completely naked, they began to undress too.

I was completely in awe of both dicks because both would fill me up. I had always thought that white guys had small ones, but looking at the white dick in front of me, I knew it was just a myth. "Get down on your knees and take these charges like a big girl." I did just as I was told and dropped to my knees. I could feel the twigs digging into them but pushed it to the back of my mind. The only thing I wanted to concentrate on now was the two big twigs in front of me.

I grabbed both of them, and with one in each hand, I started to jack them simultaneously, causing pre-cum to seep out from the little holes on the tips. I brought their dicks together and pushed my tongue in between them and let the pre-cum absorb. We were deep in the woods where a cool breeze was rustling through the trees, but somehow I still managed to break out in a sweat. "Go ahead and put it in your mouth," the white officer said as he looked down at me.

As I continued to jack the black dick, I pulled the white one in between my lips. His pink flesh felt different from what I was used to. For some reason, it felt smoother. I moaned as I sucked on the head of him, "Mmm."

As he held on to my hair, the black officer got on his knees behind me and began kissing my back. I felt him slide a finger in between my thighs and flinched when he found my clit. I sucked on the white officer's dick harder while my clit was under siege. "Yeah, that feels good, suck it faster and make it cum," the white one said as he slammed into my mouth.

"Mmm. Mmm," I moaned.

The black one jacked my clit and said, "You want me to fuck this pussy real good for you? Huh?"

"Mmm hmm," I moaned again.

I sucked the dick as if my life depended on it, and when I felt the finger enter me, I sucked even harder. I wanted the white one to cum so I could get off the ground and get fucked. As if he read my mind, he cried out, "Yeah, don't stop." Not even thirty seconds later, he went still and I felt his hot liquid hit the back of my throat. I sucked and swallowed until he was empty, and then he pulled out. I leaned into the black officer behind me and put my hands up around his neck. He brought a hand in front of me now and pulled on my clit. The white officer said, "Damn, man. That was some good ass head. You better get yours." He then leaned against the police car to re-gain his composure.

"Come on and get up. Let me put you in the back seat. I want to be able to get up in it real good," the officer said as he let go of my clit and stood up. He reached his hand out to help me off the ground, and the leaves and twigs stuck to my knees as I rose. It was almost as if they were scared to let go, but they weren't invited to my rendezvous, so I brushed them off. We walked to the back door of the car, and when the black officer opened it, I started to sit down. He stopped me and said, "Nah, let me hit it from behind."

I was going to give it to him however he asked because he was making my dreams a reality. "Whatever you say, Of-ficer," I said as I got back up in submission.

I crawled in, this time head first, and then lay the top of my body down. The arch in my back was deep as my ass cheeks spread apart. I was ready for the dick but felt his tongue instead. "Oh, yes, mmm hmm, that feels good," I stated as he licked the wrinkles around my asshole.

"Damn, this ass tastes so good," he said right before he pushed a finger inside of me. I rotated my hips to the rhythm of his finger but was getting frustrated.

"I need something bigger to fill me up."

He pulled his finger out and said, "Oh yeah? I think I may have just what you need."

He stood up and got behind me and grabbed my hips. I could feel the head of his dick poking at my entrance, and then it slowly went in. "Ugh, yeah," I said as his width opened me right up.

He was so big I could feel the pressure of him all the way to my brain. I squinted my eyes in pleasurable pain as he hit my walls and opened me. "Is that dick too much for you?" he asked between thrusts but didn't ease up.

"Uh, uh. That dick feels good. Fuck me harder," I responded as his balls swung back and forth. "Damn, this is some good dick," I said as the other car door opened. I had been so into the dick that I had forgotten about the white officer sitting outside. I must have sucked him off really good, because it took a long time for him to reappear.

"You alright in here, partner?" he asked as the black man tore my pussy up.

"Yeah, man. You should hit this one good time before we haul her in," the one inside of me said as I felt his dick begin to pulse.

I knew that he was on the verge of cumming and wanted to cum with him. "Oh, yes, yes, I'm gonna cum with you," I cried out as I reached down and stimulated my clit. Not even a minute later, my pussy juice squirted out and covered him.

"Ah shit. Ah, ah," he yelled right after I came, and then pulled out, breathing heavily and backed up, putting his hands on his knees.

I looked up and asked the white officer, "What's the matter? Don't you want a little bit too?"

He smiled and got in the back seat with me. I got up to give him room. He said, "I want some of that ass." I rubbed my hand in the cum that the other officer left behind and then rubbed it into my ass crack so it would be good and lubricated. I then got up and positioned myself on the white man's lap with my back to him. I locked my finger around the metal of the grill between the front and back seats and slightly lifted. I pushed my ass back to him and closed my eyes as he entered me. It had been a long time since I had been fucked in the ass, and I had always enjoyed it. The man held on to my hips and pushed up as I pushed down. "Yeah. That's what I'm talking about," he said as he watched his dick put in work.

"Mmm hmmm. It does feel good! Yes," I said as I continued to ride. He then let my hips go and reached around to touch my breasts. I gripped the metal tighter as he pinched my nipples, bringing me to another orgasm. "Oh my god. I'm gonna cum again. Oh shit. Oh, oh," I said as I went faster.

Suddenly, he squeezed my breasts really hard and said, "I'm cumming in this ass. Yeah, keep riding it. I'm cumming." He squeezed even harder as he filled my asshole with his liquid pleasure. He didn't let go until he was done. When he finally pulled out of me, we all got cleaned up and dressed.

They secured my wrists with the cuffs again and put me in the back of the car. "Sorry, but we got to take you in. The chief wants to see you," the white officer told me as he slammed the back door.

When I got out of the car, they escorted me to the chief's office. I felt like every eye in the building was focused on me, so I made sure to switch my hips a little harder. The officers staring was fine, and I imagined them all running a train on me. A dick could fill every hole in my body and also my hands. I'd never had more than two men at one time and wondered what more would be like. The thoughts made me wet as I looked back at each one of them. There was only one female among them, and when I looked into her eyes, I winked. I wondered how many of them she had already fucked and felt a little jealous. Nobody spoke to me as I was taken through, but I could read their thoughts, and they resembled mine.

"Okay, we're here. If you want to walk out of here, then I suggest you act accordingly," the officer told me before knocking on the chief's door.

When the door opened, my clit almost popped out of my panties. I was looking at the sexiest brother I had ever seen. His Caesar cut fit perfectly around the edge of his face. His lips were full and heart shaped, and I could already feel them on my clit. I was so enthralled that I didn't hear a word he said. I only saw his lips move, and then the sound of the door slamming broke me from my trance. "I'm going to take the cuffs off of you now. Please don't make me have to use force," he said in his deep baritone. I sat down in the chair he pointed to as he went around his desk and began to shuffle papers around. "I see you have some unpaid fines, which is why you were brought in. Can you take care of those today?"

"Yes, yes, I can," I responded with a slight nervousness in my voice.

"And you are going to pay for those how?" he questioned, as I felt my heartrate speed up.

"Well, sir, I was hoping to make some kind of trade in order to gain some leniency," I said as I slid up to the edge of my seat and pulled my skirt up enough to show my thighs.

He lifted his eyebrows and then leaned back in his chair. I watched as he rubbed his dick and asked, "Hmm, leniency? How lenient would you like me to be?"

I stood from the chair I was sitting in and walked around his desk. I stood in front of him and lifted my skirt up so he could see my pussy. It seemed as if my clit had grown in size as I touched it and asked, "I don't know. How lenient can you be?"

He stood from his chair and towered over me, but his huge presence didn't cause me to bow down. I was confident and knew that my pussy had the power to tame him. I didn't say anything else as I reached and unzipped his slacks. His dick was so big that I ended up having to undo his belt and all to pull it out. I knew that I wouldn't be able to take all of it in my mouth, but I was going to take what I could. Right before I bent over, he said, "Let's see how much of this fine you're going to pay off."

I then opened my mouth as much as I could and pulled his head in. He filled my mouth as much as he could as I sucked like never before. "Yeah, just like that," he said over me as he placed his hand on my back and rotated his hips.

My mouth grew tired quickly, so I let him fall out of it and planted my ass on his desk and said, "Come fuck me with that big motherfucker." I could prepare myself for the intrusion. I hoped that he wouldn't rip me apart. He put his anaconda dick to my hole and pushed in roughly. He showed me no remorse as he filled me up. "Holy shit," I blurted out as I almost lost my breath.

He stated, "This too much dick for you? Huh?"

"No, no, I love it. Fuck this pussy real good."

He held my legs up by the ankles as he plunged into me. "Damn, this some good pussy," he said seductively as his balls slapped me on the ass.

168

"Oh shit. Oh shit. Oh shit," I cried out in pleasure and pain as he fucked me hard.

It didn't take but a few minutes for him to say, "I'm gonna cum. I'm cumming." And then he pulled out and came all over my pussy and said, "Your fine is now paid in full. You're free to leave."

I was a little disappointed because I thought he would last longer, but I didn't sweat it too much. Instead, I got off the desk, fixed my clothes, and without saying a word, I walked out.

The sirens behind me brought me out of my daydream, and I realized that I was speeding. I looked in my rearview at the police car behind me and decided I better pull over. I found a side street and slowed down before finally coming to a complete stop. I shut off the engine and opened my glove box to retrieve the necessary paperwork I knew they would ask for. Once I got the papers, I sat back up and rolled my window down. When I looked up, I saw two officers looking down at me, one black and one white, as they said, "Ma'am, we're going to need you to step out of the car."

Sugar E. Walls

Chapter Fourteen

Explored Ecstasy

The first time I heard his voice, it made me forget anyone else before him. I felt something that I had never felt before. I felt an instant connection. He had been a stranger to me but deep inside, it felt like he had always been a part of my life. I tried to fight it but I lost the battle, because our chemistry was off the charts.

He was the most handsome man I had ever laid eyes on. His imperfections made him oh so perfect. He was five nine with smooth brown skin and brown eyes so deep you'd mistake them for black. Not only did we have great conversations, but he made me laugh with each of them. He also made me wet. I had never met a man who could match my sexual desires, but I felt like he could be the one to keep up with me. I had to have him at least once because I needed to find out what intrigued me so much. I only had pictures of this man, but we would meet very soon.

"What about this weekend?" he asked as a smile spread across my lips.

I answered, "Okay, this weekend is perfect. I'll see you then." I was overdue for some affection and longed for it so bad. It seemed like forever since I'd had some dick, so I was going to make it count. I had felt neglected for so long, but there was something more leading me to this man, something that I couldn't deny nor run from. It was slowly pulling me more and more into him each day.

The week took forever to pass by, and I found it hard to sleep at night. I would have to dive into a good book until it made me drowsy enough to knock out. The closer the weekend got, the more excited I became. Thinking about him and wondering what his touch felt like had me so horny, so I decided to use it to my advantage the next time we talked. "Do you know how you make me feel when I hear your voice?" I asked him seductively.

He responded, "Nah, but why don't you tell me?"

"Hmmm, I guess I could share a little something with you," I said as I rubbed on my nipples. I put him on speaker phone, so I could keep it real, and started. "You make my nipples so hard they hurt," I said as I continued to molest my breasts.

Before I said anything else, he interrupted me, "Hey, why don't let you let me guide you. It may help you get through till the weekend."

"Okay, go ahead," I said in response and waited.

"Do you have any clothes on?" he asked hungrily.

I pulled my T-shirt from over my head and my panties off and said, "Okay, now I'm naked." And then the games began.

"I want you to put your fingers around your nipples and pull on them gently." I did as he said and closed my eyes as he continued. "I want you to push one of them up and run your tongue across it." He paused as I licked my nipple.

"Mmm," I moaned at the feeling.

"I want you to imagine that it's my tongue. It's long and wet, and as I suck your nipple into my mouth, a little of my spit dribbles down to your stomach." It felt like I could really feel his tongue. He continued, "Now, I want you to spread your legs. Let me know when they're open." He stopped talking as he waited for me to respond.

I spread my legs and said to him, "Okay, they're open now." I was already breathing heavy when he began to talk again.

"Take your middle finger and place it on that fat clit and press down as hard as you can."

I took my middle finger and put it between my legs. My clit was already poking out from my pussy lips. I put my finger on it and pressed. "Oh god, yes! Oh shit. Ugh, ugh," I cried out from the pressure. My clit beat like a drum was inside of it as his voice carried on.

"Don't let up off of that pretty pearl, but I want you to move your finger in a circle while you hold it there."

I listened, and when the first circle was made, I thought I was going to explode. I knew it wouldn't be long before I came. "Mmm. Mmm hmm, yes," I moaned from the sensation

"Now I want you to move that same finger down your pussy slit until you get to the hole. I know it's wet by now, but I want you to touch it and tell me how wet you are."

I slowly moved my finger off my clit and pushed it farther down. My pussy was wetter than it had ever been, and he hadn't even touched it yet because he had me doing it for him. I told him what he wanted to hear, "Oh my god, my pussy is so fucking wet. Shit."

He then said, "Push your finger in the wetness and push in and out a few times. Wet that finger up." He paused and then said, "You got it in there. Huh? Answer me."

"Yes, yes. Oh my god, yes, it's in there," I cried out.

Then he said, "Now act like it's my long, fat finger. Can you feel it slide in and out of that pussy? Damn, that pussy is so wet. I'm about to suck on that pretty pearl. Are you ready?"

"Please, yes. Please suck it," I said between moans.

"Now I'm flicking my tongue over it. That bitch is fat. Can you feel me sucking it?" he asked, and I couldn't find the voice to answer him, so he asked again. "I said, can you feel me sucking that bitch? Answer me."

I finally answered, "Yes. Oh god, I'm gonna cum. Holy shit. I'm gonna cum."

"Uh, uh, pull that finger out and put it back on that clit and jack that bitch," he said in a demanding voice.

I pulled my finger out and it was covered in my pussy juice. I placed it back over my clit and started back with the circular motions. "I'm doing it. I'm on my clit," I said to him.

He said back, "Now make that little bitch cum for me. Go ahead. Make it cum. Come on, come on."

"Yeah, yeah, I'm cumming. I'm fucking cumming."

"Don't stop, keep that finger going. Don't stop until you're through. Is that pussy squirting for me? Tell me what it's doing."

"It's…it's squirting, yes. Oh shit. Aaaaagh." I came so hard I thought I would go into cardiac arrest. I swear I needed an oxygen machine right then. "Uh, uh. Oh god. Oh, uh." I breathed heavily as his voice came back over the phone.

"Did that feel good? Mmm, mmm, mmm. I can't wait to get up in that pussy and make you really feel me." I was so shocked at how easily he made me cum. I knew right then that as soon as he touched me, I wouldn't be able to handle it. He asked, "How do you feel?"

I was actually a little embarrassed that I did that over the speaker phone. I had never even imagined in my wildest dreams doing what I had just done. I finally answered, "I cannot believe I just did that. Oh my god, it was so wonderful. I can't wait to see what you have in store for me this weekend."

He said, "Yeah, ma, I hope you're ready. I'll see you then."

After we hung up, I just lay there for a minute because I couldn't do anything else. All of my energy was spent, and I was so glad it was spent on him. I knew that he was going to fuck me so good this weekend, and I couldn't wait.

I finally found the will to get up and went to take a shower. When the water hit my most intimate parts, it caused me to flinch because every part was still so sensitive. When I went to wash myself, the feeling almost knocked me off my feet. "Oh my goodness," I said out loud to myself, because I was just so amazed at how he affected me. When I got out of the shower, I went to lay down without putting on my night clothes. Hell, I was too exhausted to do anything, so I just closed my eyes and fell into a deep sleep.

The morning came so fast it was as if the night had never existed. I opened my eyes at the sound of the alarm clock and hit the snooze button immediately. I wanted to stay in bed until the weekend came, which was only two days away. I heard someone knock at my door and hoped that they would go away if I didn't answer, but they were persistent and continued knocking. I finally got up and put my robe around me to go see who fucked up my day. I opened the door to a delivery man with six roses and a small package. I looked at him with confused eyes and asked, "Um, wow, are you sure you have the right apartment?"

He smiled and said, "Yes, ma'am. This is 4-B and these are supposed to be delivered to 4-B, so yep. It's correct."

I took the flowers and the box and thanked him before I shut the door. I went back to my bedroom and sat on the bed before I read the card attached to the flowers. It read, "I'll give you the other half of these when we meet this weekend. Enjoy your gift. Call me as soon as you open it."

I smiled from ear to ear and then pulled the bow off the box to open it. Inside was a long black dildo, and when I saw it, I was speechless. This man was freaky, and that shit turned me on completely. I immediately picked up the phone and called him, and he answered on the first ring. "I take it since you're calling me you got your gifts," he said, and although I couldn't see his face, I could feel him smiling.

I said to him, "Yes, I did get them, and now I'm wondering what exactly you want me to do with this."

He said to me, "Get undressed."

I responded, "Already done, now what?"

"Lay back and spread your legs. Act like I'm in front of you," he told me aggressively, and, of course, I did as he said.

I positioned myself with my back leaned against my headboard with my legs spread as wide as I could get them, and then I asked, "Okay, what now?"

"Get your laptop out and put us on Facetime. I want you to sit it right in front of the pussy," he said to me. I leaned over and got my laptop off my nightstand and opened it. I put the screen on Facetime, and his handsome face popped up. I put my phone down and waited for him to speak. "Damn, that pussy is nice and juicy. Spread it open for me,"

I was a freaky bitch, but I had never done no freaky shit like this. All I knew was that I liked it. I spread my pussy lips apart and asked him, "Do you know what to do with something like this?"

He laughed and said, "Nah, the question is, does something like that know what to do with me?" I couldn't help but laugh at his humor and was ready to begin whatever adventure he had for me. He asked, "Are you ready for me to give you what you need?"

"Yes. I've been ready," I said, and then he started up.

"I want you to take that big black dick I sent you today and rub it down the middle of that wet pussy." I did as he said as he watched me from the screen. "Yea, just like that," he said as my pussy lips caressed the dark toy. He asked, "How does that feel?"

I said, "Hmmm. It feels so good, but I'm sure not as good as the real thing."

"Don't worry, ma, this big black dick is gonna be in that pussy soon enough." I continued to rub the dildo down in my folds until he said, "Now, I want you to take the head of it and push it in that pussy. Do it slow, though."

I turned the dildo so I could get a better grip on it and put it at my entrance. I looked into his eyes and then slowly pushed it in. The head of the dildo had little ridges around it, and when it rubbed against my hole, it caused me to flinch and moan in pleasure, "Oh, mmm, shit."

"Yeah, you like that shit, huh? I want you to close your eyes now and imagine that it's me going up in you instead. Can you do that for me?" he asked as he instructed me of my next move.

I told him, "Yes," as I closed my eyes.

"Now, I want you to push it a little further and then pull it out, leaving only the head inside."

I then pushed it back in. I kept doing it until I could maintain a steady rhythm. "Mmm, yes. It feels so good," I said aloud as I sped up.

I heard him say, "Yeah, baby, take that dick and make that pussy cum. I want you to cum all over that dick. Fuck that pussy, baby, yes."

The more he spoke, the faster I went. Had I not been holding it, I probably would have gotten lost inside my walls. "Oh, yes, yes, oh, I'm gonna cum. I'm gonna cum all over this dick, yes. Yes," I cried out as the feeling overtook me.

I could feel myself getting dizzy and knew that I was about to let it all out. "Come on, cum for me. Come on. Let me see that pussy squirt," he said, and no sooner than he did, I began to cum.

"Mmm, yes. Uh huh, yeah, oh yeah," I moaned as my juices covered the fake dick.

"Yeah, that's what I'm talking about. I want that same shit all over my dick. Damn, I can't wait to taste you. I bet you taste as sweet as pie." After I finished cumming, I pulled the dildo out and for special effects, I put it in my mouth and sucked my cum off of it. It drove him totally crazy. He said, "Damn, you just made a nigga shoot his shit everywhere. You fucked me up with that one."

I laughed and said, "Don't worry. I got you."

We ended our Facetime, and then I lay back down. I lay in the bed and thought about him all day and wondered what he would think of next. He already had my mind, and the way he had my body feeling, I knew that he would soon possess my heart too. The time passed and I waited all day to hear from him, but nothing came through. I had only this day left before we would actually meet. I hoped nothing happened to prevent our inevitable meeting. I decided to get up and get something to eat and then take a shower, but as soon as I left my bedroom, I heard my phone ring. I knew that it was him before I even answered because I could always feel his closeness.

"Hello," I said when I answered. As soon as I heard his voice, I became wet.

"Hey, as soon as the sun comes up, be ready. Have an overnight bag, because I ain't trying to rush to get you back." And then he hung up.

"Oh, don't worry, I'll be ready," I said to myself with a smile as I proceeded with what I was doing. When I got back in my bed, I went right to sleep. I wanted the morning to hurry and get here.

I forgot to set my alarm because my mind was so focused on him, so a sudden knock at my door was what woke me up.

I looked at the clock and said frantically, "Oh my god, I can't fucking believe this. No, not today of all days."

The knocking continued as I tried to make myself presentable, but I knew I had to answer the door. When I opened it, there he was in all his glory. I was speechless because in person, he was even more handsome. He had me mesmerized and not to mention, so, so wet.

"You gonna let me in, or you just gonna stand there and stare at me?" he asked and broke me out of my trance.

"Oh, I'm sorry. I am so sorry. Come on in," I said as I opened the door further to allow him access. I said, "Um, make yourself comfortable. As you can see, I'm running a little late."

He walked to the couch and sat down as I ran into the bathroom to hurry and get myself together. While I was in the shower rinsing my body, I heard the bathroom door open, and then the shower curtain slid back. "Don't mind me. I'm just admiring a beautiful woman." I stopped breathing for a few seconds and then reached for the towel.

As I dried off, he stared at me and said nothing, and then suddenly, he reached out and ran a finger over my nipple. "Ugh," was all I could manage to get out.

He smiled at me and said, "Don't worry, I'm saving what I got for you until later." And then he walked out of the bathroom and left me standing there dumbfounded. I finally finished drying off and then went to get dressed and pack my bag.

We didn't speak the entire ride but just held hands in anticipation of what was about to go down. He finally pulled into the driveway of a beautiful home. Everything outside was immaculate, so I knew the inside would be the same. When we got to the front door, he leaned down and kissed me on the cheek before he opened the door. When I walked in, he said,

"Your other six roses," and held his hand out. There were rose petals all over the floor. I stood there in amazement, and then he said, "Follow them." And I did.

The rose petals led me to his bedroom and circled the king-size bed. The room was dimly lit and soft music was playing. When I turned around, I almost hit him because he was right up on me. Before I even had a chance to speak, he leaned down and pulled my bottom lip into his mouth. The chill bumps formed instantly and almost brought me to my knees. When our kiss broke, he put his hand under my chin and lifted so that my eyes met his, and said, "You ready for this?"

I said to him, "I've been ready." He grabbed the strap of my sundress and pulled it down as he lightly kissed my shoulder, and then he did the other one the same way. "Mmm," I moaned from his touch. He then pushed the straps further and made my dress fall in a heap at my feet. He ran a finger over the front of my strapless bra, making my nipples instantly react and point straight at him. He bent down and pulled one between his lips, wetting the fabric that separated him from it. I held my head back and when I did, I noticed glowing stars on the ceiling giving the room an outside ambiance. He finally reached his hands around my back and unsnapped the bra, letting it fall over the dress on the floor. He then turned me around so that my back faced him and started by planting small kisses across my back, shoulder to shoulder. "That feels nice," I said as I leaned my head down.

He brought his hands around and traced my nipples with his soft hands. His touch was so sensual and so inviting. "Mmm, yes," I moaned as his hands then disappeared and fell to my hips. He latched a finger on each side of my bikini-cut panties and went down to his knees as he slid them from my hips. When they got to my feet, I stepped out of them one foot at a time. I still had my heels on, and he removed them after he threw my panties to the side. Before he came back up, he placed his hands on my ass cheeks and slightly spread them apart. When I felt his tongue slide through my crack, I almost lost all composure. "Oh my god. Shit," I cried out as he ran his tongue from the bottom to the top and then came back up.

"Come on. Let's go to the bed. I want to taste you," he said so sensually and deep.

He walked behind me and held on to my shoulders until we got there, and then he turned me around to face him. He pulled his shirt from over his head and when he went to unbuckle his pants, I reached out to assist him. "Let me," I said as I unbuttoned and then unzipped them. I could see the bulge before I even pushed them down and knew right then that my pussy was going to be completely satisfied. When I pulled his pants down, his bulge seemed to grow bigger, but I was not going to let that stop me. I noticed a small wet spot on his boxer briefs from the pre-cum that had formed. I grabbed the rim of his briefs and pulled them down too and was almost knocked out by his hardness.

It was about eight inches long and nice and thick. He saw me looking and asked, "You think you can handle that?" I looked up at him and smiled and without saying a word. I pulled the head of his dick into my mouth. I could still taste his pre-cum and it aroused my senses even more. "Mmm. That shit feels good, ma," he said as he slowly rotated his hips. I held the length of him in my hand as I sucked his hardness. I then felt him pull back as he said, "Nah, I ain't cumming like this." And then he reached his hands under my arm pits and pulled me up from the floor. He got on the bed and sat up with his back pressed against the headboard and said, "Come here and let me taste that honey." I got on the bed with him and stood up to straddle his face. I put my hands against the wall and inhaled a deep breath when I felt him pull my clit into his warm mouth.

He sucked on my clit slow and hard and then pushed a finger inside of me. I knew it wouldn't take me long to cum because the feeling was so intense. I looked down at him at the same time he looked up at me and watched him do his thing. "Yes, oh my god, you're about to make me cum. Yes, it feels so good," I cried out in pleasure as he brought me to ecstasy. My knees began to get weak and my mind got dizzy. I knew that I was about to rain on him, so I said, "I'm gonna cum. Yes. Oh yes. I'm cumming." No sooner than I said it, my cum squirted out and covered his chin. I tried to pull away, but he had a strong grip on me. "Oh, oh shit. Oh fuck. Oh," I screamed out as my clit became numb. He didn't stop until I finished cumming.

When he finally let me go, I squatted down over him. I needed to catch my breath before I gave him the ride of his life. I wrapped my arms around his neck and latched my fingers together. He asked, "Did you like that?"

I answered, "Yes. That shit almost knocked me off my feet. It was so damn good." We shared a small laugh and then kissed. I was ready to have his dick inside of me. He looked me in the eyes as he wrapped his hand around his thickness and held it up. I put my pussy directly over it and invited him in. "Oh yes," I said as his head penetrated my opening. I had to go down on it slow because it had been such a long time for me, but once he was all the way in there, I rode out like a soldier.

"Damn, this pussy feels good on my dick," he said as he brought his hands around me and held on to my ass cheeks.

He would push up as I pushed down and met me thrust for thrust. "Oh yes. Mmm hmm. Yes. I'm gonna make this dick cum so hard," I said as his dick filled my walls.

I could feel his dick pulsating and knew that he was ready to fill me up. He cried out, "You 'bout to make this dick cum. Shit, you feel so damn good." As soon as he said it, I began to ride him faster. The echo of our bodies meeting filled the room and then suddenly, he gripped my ass cheeks and pushed into me one final time so he could release everything I deserved. "Ugh, ugh, shit, ugh." He breathed heavily as I rotated my hips and let him fill me to capacity.

After he came, I kissed him and got up. He lay down and pulled me beside him. I lay my head down on his chest as he wrapped an arm around me. I knew that this was where we would be for the rest of the day and on into the night. As we lay there for a few minutes, he finally broke the silence and said, "Damn, that was worth the wait."

Chapter Fifteen

A Brewing Storm

There was a storm brewing in the distance. I could feel it all through my body and could already smell the scent of the rain in the air. The news said that it would be a ferocious one, and when they did, my adrenaline spiked. I had always loved the sound of the rain as it pattered onto the ground and sent the leaves afloat. The sound of the thunder and the strike of lightning as they accompanied it. The wind blowing fiercely as the tree limbs swayed side to side. I had always dreamed of sitting outside as the skies pushed their wrath upon the earth's surface. Naked, I would lay under the trees as the tiny droplets pounded onto my skin. I decided that I would make my dreams reality.

I went into my kitchen and grabbed my picnic basket so I could fill it up with all the things I would need. I put in a wine glass and a bottle of my favorite Chardonnay along with some strawberries and whipped cream. I went to my bedroom and grabbed my eight-inch dildo because he was about to put in some work. I also grabbed a comforter and a plastic spread sheet to put under it so the leaves and twigs wouldn't stick to it. I didn't care about it getting wet because I wanted to enjoy the wetness of it against my skin. I then stripped out of all my clothing and wrapped my robe around myself. One of the perks of doing this was that I didn't have any neighbors for a couple of miles, so I didn't have to worry about offending anyone.

After I had everything ready, I slipped on a pair of my beach shoes and went outside to wait on the storm. I placed the plastic sheet on the ground and then put the comforter on top of it. I took out my Chardonnay and glass and poured me some out and set it beside me. Next were my strawberries and cream and then my favorite toy. No sooner than I had everything out, I heard thunderclap in the distance and knew that I wouldn't have to wait much longer.

I drank a little wine, and as I started to eat the strawberries, I felt the first drop. The wind blew hard and made my nipples react. They stood at attention, as if saluting the drops. I untied my robe and leaned back against the tree.

I decided to have a little extra fun before it came full force, so I got the whipped cream and squirted a little on each of my nipples. I then pushed my breasts together and stuck my tongue out. I lifted my breasts and licked the whipped cream off. "Mmm," I moaned as I felt more drops hitting my skin.

About that time, I heard a car pull up in my driveway. I looked and saw that it was my man, and when he noticed me sitting under the tree, he asked, "Baby, what the hell are you doing?"

I told him seductively, "Get naked and join me. I wanna get fucked in the rain." He looked crazy, but I knew how to persuade him. I picked up my dildo and spread my legs. I then squirted some of the cream on the dildo's head and put it in my mouth. I said, "You mean to tell me you're gonna let this dick right here have all the fun?"

I ran the dildo down the length of my body and then between my pussy lips. I looked up at his crotch area and noticed that his dick was getting hard. He licked his lips and said, "Come on, ma, let's take this shit inside."

The drops of rain tripled and were starting to come down at a steady pace. I said, "Come on, baby. I've always wanted to do this. No one else can see us, so pull that dick out and handle your business."

The thunder roared as I put the head of the dildo to my pussy hole and pushed it inside. "Damn, ma. I can't believe you doing this shit," he said as he started to strip. The rain pelted down in a steady pour now as the lightning streaked across the sky. I laughed as he took his clothes off in the pouring rain. "What if we get struck by lightning out here?" he asked.

I responded, "All it will do is give us an extra burst of energy, babe."

He fell to his knees and leaned over to kiss me. I caressed his face as he sucked my tongue into his mouth. The wine and strawberries were long forgotten, replaced by the pleasure of his presence. He reached for the dildo still in my grasp and pulled it from me. "You won't be needing that," he said as the rain drops hit his lips. Little droplets clung to his eyelashes, as if they were afraid to let go. "Honey, it's pouring fucking rain out here. Let's go inside," he said, but I wasn't trying to hear it. I pushed him back on his ass and immediately pulled his dick between my lips. My ass was up and slightly spread as the rain fell through the crack of it, stimulating my nerves.

I could feel the rain attacking my folds as I deep throated him. "Mmm. Damn, ma, you wild as fuck," he said as I sucked him harder. The rain blurred my vision as the sky clapped at my performance. My hair was soaked and tickled his balls as I pulled him deeper. "Damn, you gonna make me cum," he said as he placed a hand on the back of my head and pushed up. The harder the rain fell, the harder I sucked his length. "I'm about to cum, ma. You ready for this shit? Huh?" he said.

Without letting him go, I answered. "Mmm hmm." I was ready to swallow it.

"Baby, shit," he said, right before his creamy essence shot out. I sucked and swallowed at the same time until there was nothing left.

I felt a little deprived because I wanted him inside of me, but sooner than later, I would get him back right so he could fill me up. In the meantime, I was going to use my trusty little friend. I let his dick fall from my mouth as the rain steadily poured. "You cheated me, but I'm gonna get mine anyway." I sat up and leaned back against the tree again, and as I spread my pussy lips open, the rain pounded on my clit. "Oh, baby, come over here and suck my pussy for me," I begged him, and he didn't hesitate. He licked the rain off me from my ankle to my thigh, right before his tongue found my swollen clit. "Here, baby, use this," I said as I handed him the dildo.

I could tell he felt some type of way, but I needed something to hold me over until his dick was hard again. He reluctantly took it out my hand, and as he sucked my clit into his mouth, he slowly pushed the length of the toy inside of me. I put both of my hands on the back of his head and thrusted my pussy into his face. I leaned my head up some and opened my mouth so the rainwater could quench the thirst that had built up. When my mouth got full, I spit it out and let it roll down over my breasts. "Yes, baby, that feels so good. Yes, make me cum. Work that dick and make me cum," I said to him loudly, because the rain was pouring harder and trying to block out my words. The droplets stung as they hit my body, and I welcomed the pain because it felt too good to ignore.

He sucked on my clit with attitude, and I knew deep down that he only went along with this escapade to please me. He was making my clit numb with the pressure he placed upon it. Pushing the dildo into me hard, he would then pull it out slow. I was on the verge of an orgasm and needed him to know it, so I yelled out, "I'm cumming. Shit, I'm cumming. Yes, baby, yes." He pulled the dildo out as soon as I said it because he only wanted my juices in his mouth, not on some foreign object. "Oh yes, yes," I cried out one last time, before I stiffened up and squirt my cum onto his chin. Before the rain could wash my creamy filling away, he stuck his tongue in my hole. He kept it in there until he absorbed every drop of flavor.

When I was done, he looked up at me and said, "Turn that ass over. You wanna get fucked in pouring down rain, I'm gonna give you some real dick." I smiled because I knew he meant what he said. I turned over and arched my back so my ass would be in the air, and he wasted no time pushing up in me. "This what the fuck you want?" he asked as he pushed into me hard, water causing my ass to sting every time he slammed against me.

His balls were swinging not only from the force of his movement but also from the force of the wind. The thunder in the sky threatening the ground we fucked on made it tremble. "Yes, that's just what I want. Fuck me harder," I said while I enjoyed the length of him inside me.

All of a sudden, I felt his thumb enter my asshole, and it caused me to back against him more aggressively. The lightning streaked across the sky and caused a shot of electricity to flow through me. "Oh yes, mmm hmmm. I'm gonna cum. I'm cumming." No sooner than I said it, my pussy began to squirt once again. This time, he let it be over his dick.

He pulled his thumb out of me and grabbed my hips so he could prepare himself for another explosion. "Shit, shit, shit, I'm cumming," he yelled out over the rain, and then he pulled out of me and came all over my ass cheeks. The rain quickly washed it away.

I lay down on my stomach, and he lay down on top of me and asked, "You better now?"

I turned over, making him roll off of me, and answered, "Yes, now wasn't that fun?"

He just shook his head and lay it down on the cover. The rain then started to slow, as if it had waited until we fulfilled what we were there to do. I looked down at his dick as the coolness of the air made it shrink. I rolled over on my side and lay my head on his chest and put my hand over his dick to keep it warm. When the rain completely stopped, we shared a laugh, and he said, "I cannot believe we just did that shit. But damn, it was great." He kissed the top of my head and asked, "Can we get up off this wet ass ground now?"

I pinched his nipple. "Yeah, we are going to catch pneumonia from this, and honestly babe, it will be well worth it." He got up and pulled me up with him. He helped me gather the things I had brought out so we could carry them back inside. When we got in, we dried off and put on some dry clothes so we could warm up.

I made us cups of hot cocoa and we sat in front of the television and cuddled up. He turned on the news and the weather report was showing the next day's forecast. We looked at each other and laughed when the newscaster said, "Tomorrow, a storm will be brewing."

Chapter Sixteen

Just a Peek

I watched through their window as she sucked his uncircumcised dick into her mouth. The way she pulled the skin back and made his mushroom-shaped head pop out had my panties wet. I moaned as she licked around the head delicately with the tip of her tongue. I could see his pre-cum glistening in the dim light, until she finally swiped it away and savored the flavor. "Mmm. Damn," I said in a low voice carefully so no one would hear me.

His dick was long and skinny, and it disappeared in her mouth like a snake going into a hole to hide in the earth. He closed his eyes and put a hand on the back of her head and pushed his pelvis into her. "Damn," I said as I slid my tiny hand into my panties. I had been doing this for a while, and they never disappointed me with their performance. I sometimes wondered if they knew I was there watching them, or if they really felt like they were alone enjoying an intimate moment.

She sped up as I watched his lips move and say something. I couldn't hear him, though, because the breeze of the night stole the words I so desperately needed. She continued to deep throat him as her breasts swung under her, the nipples hard and brushing up against the fabric of the sheet. I could imagine the sensation it gave her every time the roughness caressed the tips of them. I knew that soon, he would cum and she would swallow every drop. None was ever wasted. I could tell she enjoyed the taste of him and savored every drop. When he stiffened, I knew he was cumming. The veins in his muscles popped up to help him relieve the pressure. She slowed down as his seeds flowed down her throat. "Ugh, ugh," I grunted as I touched the inner folds of my most precious place. My pearl was hard and throbbed like a heartbeat. I knew the next scene was about to begin, and I wanted to be ready.

She let him fall from her mouth, and as his newly soft dick plopped down on his thigh, she rose. It was her turn until he got back right. They switched places, and now instead of her nipples brushing the sheets, they stood erect and look toward the ceiling. They were plump and my mouth watered at the thought of running my tongue around one. I wouldn't be greedy with it, just a slow, short lick, and then I'd move on, but I didn't get that chance because he already had one held hostage between his lips. He sucked so hard his cheeks sank in, and my nipples rose and poked out through my shirt. They strained against it, as if they were trying to get him to suck them too. It was painful, but the pain was welcome.

I pressed on my clit as he released the nipple and made a trail of kisses to her navel. His tongue stopped and went around her navel before moving on. Her legs were spread and ready, and her pussy, oh, her pussy was so perfectly trimmed and formed. I was a little envious because it looked untouched and so, so innocent. I made slow, circular movements now as he went further and dove into the center of her universe. Her clit poked out and dared him to suck it. He showed no fear as he pulled it in between his lips. "Oh yes, mmm, suck it," I said in pleasure, as I stroked my clit up and down, seeking the release it needed so desperately.

He pushed a finger inside of her, and her wetness covered it as he went in and out. He sped up, and I felt like I could hear her crying out for him to fuck her faster. Her hips thrust as her legs slightly lifted. I felt myself on the verge of an orgasm, but I wanted to wait for her so we could cum together. I knew it wouldn't be long, so I kept moving my finger and she kept moving her hips. "Oh yes, yes, oh, oh, I'm cumming," I yelled out, not caring right then if I was heard or not. I looked, and as my cum squirted, her love juice squirted on his chin. Unbeknownst to her, we shared this moment often, and it was one I always treasured.

It was time now. I knew because I saw his dick had grown back to the size it was before. The little eye peeking out from over the skin that had protected it for so long. He got on his knees and pushed into her wet hole. He lifted her legs to his shoulders and pushed them back against her chest. I could see his dick go in and out of her hole like a drill in cement. Pump in, pump out again and again as she was pinned under him.

She took the dick like a pro and he gave it to her like he was an all-star. I could see the sweat forming on their bodies. The sheen glistening as he stroked. His ass muscles clenching in her ecstasy as he hit her walls. I said to him, although he couldn't hear me, "Yes, fuck that pussy good. Make that pussy cum again." I pushed a finger inside of me. It went so easy because I was soaking wet. Every time he pushed in, my finger did the same. I moaned to myself, "Mmm, mmm, yes." She reached her hands down and clenched his ass cheeks. I could see her nails dig into the flesh, and it let me know that the dick was good to her. "So good, yes, I know," I said as if he was inside of me too.

I swear that I could hear as their bodies slapped together, sounding like an applause from an audience. He slammed into her one last time and then backed out. I could see the head of his dick now as it erupted like a volcano. She was out of breath and still, she found the strength to hop up and catch what he was giving her. Some of it wasted, but she didn't worry about it because she knew there was plenty more where it came from.

As she drank his essence, she pumped him like a well. His balls swung and hit her chin rudely, but her mind was on bigger and better things. I cum again as she licked his head and cleaned him up, and now that she was done drinking, she finally paid closer attention to the hanging orbs. She took them in her hand and rolled them around with her fingers like stress balls. I could see her ease her other hand further back, and I wondered if he was expecting it or was it going to be a nice surprise.

As she penetrated his forbidden zone, I saw him pull back some, but he ultimately gave in and let her handle it. He seemed to like it, and I wondered what ran through his mind as she violated him. He was beginning to grow once again, and I was so in awe of his stamina. I had always wondered what they would do if they caught me out here watching and cumming every time they came. Would they invite me inside to join the escapade, or would I be hauled off in the back of a police car and read my rights? I knew I was wrong, but I didn't care.

I wanted to fuck them together or separate as long as I could, but they didn't know about me, or did they? My pussy throbbed at an astronomical speed, and I felt as if I was going to faint. This was becoming too much for me.

The penetration worked, and he was now back on target. She got on her knees and bent over until her elbows were secured on the bed, holding her up. "Oh my god," I said as my heartrate sped up. I swear that he just locked eyes with me, but I couldn't be sure.

He went back to what he was doing before he turned this way. I peeked and saw that he had spread her ass cheeks. He pushed a finger in and then pulled it out a couple of times, and then he pushed in his manhood. Her asshole sucked him in, and he moved slowly in and out of her slower than he did before he ventured there. His muscles flexed as he pushed into her, and her breasts hung and swung once again. She pushed back as he pushed forward, and their bodies intertwined in an ecstasy like no other. Suddenly, he stopped and got up off the bed. I wanted him to finish, to get one more in before I left and called it a night. I heard a noise, and the window in front of me opened. I was afraid and nervous. What would I say to these people? It was both of them, and they poked their heads out the window. They saw me, and I didn't know if I should run or just face the music. I looked up at them as they looked back at me. Two words left their mouths, "Wanna join?"

THE END!

For Now…

Lock Down Publications and Ca$h Presents assisted publishing packages.

BASIC PACKAGE $499
Editing
Cover Design
Formatting

UPGRADED PACKAGE $800
Typing
Editing
Cover Design
Formatting

ADVANCE PACKAGE $1,200
Typing
Editing
Cover Design
Formatting
Copyright registration
Proofreading
Upload book to Amazon

LDP SUPREME PACKAGE $1,500
Typing
Editing
Cover Design
Formatting
Copyright registration
Proofreading
Set up Amazon account
Upload book to Amazon

Advertise on LDP Amazon and Facebook page

***Other services available upon request. Additional charges may apply
Lock Down Publications
P.O. Box 944
Stockbridge, GA 30281-9998
Phone # 470 303-9761

Submission Guideline

Submit the first three chapters of your completed manuscript to ldpsubmissions@gmail.com, subject line: Your book's title. The manuscript must be in a .doc file and sent as an attachment. Document should be in Times New Roman, double spaced and in size 12 font. Also, provide your synopsis and full contact information. If sending multiple submissions, they must each be in a separate email.

Have a story but no way to send it electronically? You can still submit to LDP/Ca$h Presents. Send in the first three chapters, written or typed, of your completed manuscript to:

LDP: Submissions Dept
Po Box 944
Stockbridge, Ga 30281

DO NOT send original manuscript. Must be a duplicate.

Provide your synopsis and a cover letter containing your full contact information.

Thanks for considering LDP and Ca$h Presents.

<u>NEW RELEASES</u>

CONFESSIONS OF A JACKBOY II by
NICHOLAS LOCK
A GANGSTA'S KARMA 2 by FLAME
GRIMEY WAYS by RAY VINCI
A GANGSTA SAVED XMAS by MONET
DRAGUN
XMAS WITH AN ATL SHOOTER by
CA$H & DESTINY SKAI
CUM FOR ME by SUGAR E. WALLZ

STRAIGHT BEAST MODE II

De'Kari

KINGPIN KILLAZ IV

STREET KINGS III

PAID IN BLOOD III

CARTEL KILLAZ IV

DOPE GODS III

Hood Rich

SINS OF A HUSTLA II

ASAD

RICH $AVAGE II

MONEY IN THE GRAVE II

By Martell Troublesome Bolden

YAYO V

Bred In The Game 2

S. Allen

CREAM III

By Yolanda Moore

SON OF A DOPE FIEND III

HEAVEN GOT A GHETTO II

By Renta

LOYALTY AIN'T PROMISED III

By Keith Williams

I'M NOTHING WITHOUT HIS LOVE II

SINS OF A THUG II

TO THE THUG I LOVED BEFORE II

By Monet Dragun

QUIET MONEY IV

EXTENDED CLIP III

THUG LIFE IV

By **Trai'Quan**

THE STREETS MADE ME IV

By **Larry D. Wright**

IF YOU CROSS ME ONCE II

By **Anthony Fields**

THE STREETS WILL NEVER CLOSE II

By **K'ajji**

HARD AND RUTHLESS III

THE BILLIONAIRE BENTLEYS II

Von Diesel

KILLA KOUNTY II

By **Khufu**

MONEY GAME III

By **Smoove Dolla**

JACK BOYZ VERSUS DOPE BOYZ

By **Romell Tukes**

MURDA WAS THE CASE II

Elijah R. Freeman

THE STREETS NEVER LET GO II

By **Robert Baptiste**

AN UNFORESEEN LOVE III

By **Meesha**

KING OF THE TRENCHES II
by **GHOST & TRANAY ADAMS**

MONEY MAFIA II

LOYAL TO THE SOIL II

By **Jibril Williams**

QUEEN OF THE ZOO II

By **Black Migo**

THE BRICK MAN III

By King Rio

VICIOUS LOYALTY II

By Kingpen

A GANGSTA'S PAIN II

By J-Blunt

CONFESSIONS OF A JACKBOY III

By Nicholas Lock

GRIMEY WAYS II

By Ray Vinci

<u>Available Now</u>

RESTRAINING ORDER **I & II**

By **CA$H & Coffee**

LOVE KNOWS NO BOUNDARIES **I II & III**

By **Coffee**

RAISED AS A GOON I, II, III & IV

BRED BY THE SLUMS I, II, III

BLAST FOR ME I & II

ROTTEN TO THE CORE I II III

A BRONX TALE I, II, III

DUFFLE BAG CARTEL I II III IV V VI

HEARTLESS GOON I II III IV V

A SAVAGE DOPEBOY I II

DRUG LORDS I II III

CUTTHROAT MAFIA I II

KING OF THE TRENCHES

By **Ghost**

LAY IT DOWN **I & II**

LAST OF A DYING BREED I II

BLOOD STAINS OF A SHOTTA I & II III

By **Jamaica**

LOYAL TO THE GAME I II III

LIFE OF SIN I, II III

By **TJ & Jelissa**

BLOODY COMMAS I & II

SKI MASK CARTEL I II & III

KING OF NEW YORK I II,III IV V

RISE TO POWER I II III

COKE KINGS I II III IV V

BORN HEARTLESS I II III IV

KING OF THE TRAP I II

Cum For Me 8

By **T.J. Edwards**
IF LOVING HIM IS WRONG…I & II
LOVE ME EVEN WHEN IT HURTS I II III
By **Jelissa**
WHEN THE STREETS CLAP BACK I & II III
THE HEART OF A SAVAGE I II III
MONEY MAFIA
LOYAL TO THE SOIL
By **Jibril Williams**
A DISTINGUISHED THUG STOLE MY HEART I II & III
LOVE SHOULDN'T HURT I II III IV
RENEGADE BOYS I II III IV
PAID IN KARMA I II III
SAVAGE STORMS I II
AN UNFORESEEN LOVE I II
By **Meesha**
A GANGSTER'S CODE I &, II III
A GANGSTER'S SYN I II III
THE SAVAGE LIFE I II III
CHAINED TO THE STREETS I II III
BLOOD ON THE MONEY I II III
A GANGSTA'S PAIN
By **J-Blunt**
PUSH IT TO THE LIMIT
By **Bre' Hayes**
BLOOD OF A BOSS **I, II, III, IV, V**
SHADOWS OF THE GAME

205

TRAP BASTARD

By **Askari**

THE STREETS BLEED MURDER **I, II & III**

THE HEART OF A GANGSTA I II& III

By **Jerry Jackson**

CUM FOR ME I II III IV V VI VII VIII

An **LDP Erotica Collaboration**

BRIDE OF A HUSTLA **I II & II**

THE FETTI GIRLS **I, II& III**

CORRUPTED BY A GANGSTA I, II III, IV

BLINDED BY HIS LOVE

THE PRICE YOU PAY FOR LOVE I, II ,III

DOPE GIRL MAGIC I II III

By **Destiny Skai**

WHEN A GOOD GIRL GOES BAD

By **Adrienne**

THE COST OF LOYALTY I II III

By Kweli

A GANGSTER'S REVENGE **I II III & IV**

THE BOSS MAN'S DAUGHTERS I II III IV V

A SAVAGE LOVE **I & II**

BAE BELONGS TO ME I II

A HUSTLER'S DECEIT I, II, III

WHAT BAD BITCHES DO I, II, III

SOUL OF A MONSTER I II III

KILL ZONE

A DOPE BOY'S QUEEN I II III

By **Aryanna**

A KINGPIN'S AMBITON

A KINGPIN'S AMBITION **II**

I MURDER FOR THE DOUGH

By **Ambitious**

TRUE SAVAGE I II III IV V VI VII

DOPE BOY MAGIC I, II, III

MIDNIGHT CARTEL I II III

CITY OF KINGZ I II

NIGHTMARE ON SILENT AVE

By **Chris Green**

A DOPEBOY'S PRAYER

By **Eddie "Wolf" Lee**

THE KING CARTEL **I, II & III**

By **Frank Gresham**

THESE NIGGAS AIN'T LOYAL **I, II & III**

By **Nikki Tee**

GANGSTA SHYT **I II &III**

By **CATO**

THE ULTIMATE BETRAYAL

By **Phoenix**

BOSS'N UP **I , II & III**

By **Royal Nicole**

I LOVE YOU TO DEATH

By **Destiny J**

I RIDE FOR MY HITTA

I STILL RIDE FOR MY HITTA

Sugar E. Walls

By **Misty Holt**

LOVE & CHASIN' PAPER

By **Qay Crockett**

TO DIE IN VAIN

SINS OF A HUSTLA

By **ASAD**

BROOKLYN HUSTLAZ

By **Boogsy Morina**

BROOKLYN ON LOCK I & II

By **Sonovia**

GANGSTA CITY

By **Teddy Duke**

A DRUG KING AND HIS DIAMOND I & II III

A DOPEMAN'S RICHES

HER MAN, MINE'S TOO I, II

CASH MONEY HO'S

THE WIFEY I USED TO BE I II

By Nicole Goosby

TRAPHOUSE KING **I II & III**

KINGPIN KILLAZ I II III

STREET KINGS I II

PAID IN BLOOD **I II**

CARTEL KILLAZ I II III

DOPE GODS I II

By **Hood Rich**

LIPSTICK KILLAH **I, II, III**

CRIME OF PASSION I II & III

FRIEND OR FOE I II III

By **Mimi**

STEADY MOBBN' **I, II, III**

THE STREETS STAINED MY SOUL I II

By **Marcellus Allen**

WHO SHOT YA **I, II, III**

SON OF A DOPE FIEND I II

HEAVEN GOT A GHETTO

Renta

GORILLAZ IN THE BAY **I II III IV**

TEARS OF A GANGSTA I II

3X KRAZY I II

STRAIGHT BEAST MODE

DE'KARI

TRIGGADALE I II III

MURDAROBER WAS THE CASE

Elijah R. Freeman

GOD BLESS THE TRAPPERS I, II, III

THESE SCANDALOUS STREETS I, II, III

FEAR MY GANGSTA I, II, III IV, V

THESE STREETS DON'T LOVE NOBODY I, II

BURY ME A G I, II, III, IV, V

A GANGSTA'S EMPIRE I, II, III, IV

THE DOPEMAN'S BODYGAURD I II

THE REALEST KILLAZ I II III

THE LAST OF THE OGS I II III

Tranay Adams

THE STREETS ARE CALLING
Duquie Wilson
MARRIED TO A BOSS I II III
By Destiny Skai & Chris Green
KINGZ OF THE GAME I II III IV V VI
Playa Ray
SLAUGHTER GANG I II III
RUTHLESS HEART I II III
By Willie Slaughter
FUK SHYT
By Blakk Diamond
DON'T F#CK WITH MY HEART I II
By Linnea
ADDICTED TO THE DRAMA I II III
IN THE ARM OF HIS BOSS II
By Jamila
YAYO I II III IV
A SHOOTER'S AMBITION I II
BRED IN THE GAME
By S. Allen
TRAP GOD I II III
RICH $AVAGE
MONEY IN THE GRAVE I II
By Martell Troublesome Bolden
FOREVER GANGSTA
GLOCKS ON SATIN SHEETS I II
By Adrian Dulan

TOE TAGZ I II III

LEVELS TO THIS SHYT I II

By Ah'Million

KINGPIN DREAMS I II III

By Paper Boi Rari

CONFESSIONS OF A GANGSTA I II III IV

CONFESSIONS OF A JACKBOY I II

By Nicholas Lock

I'M NOTHING WITHOUT HIS LOVE

SINS OF A THUG

TO THE THUG I LOVED BEFORE

A GANGSTA SAVED XMAS

By Monet Dragun

CAUGHT UP IN THE LIFE I II III

THE STREETS NEVER LET GO

By Robert Baptiste

NEW TO THE GAME I II III

MONEY, MURDER & MEMORIES I II III

By **Malik D. Rice**

LIFE OF A SAVAGE I II III

A GANGSTA'S QUR'AN I II III

MURDA SEASON I II III

GANGLAND CARTEL I II III

CHI'RAQ GANGSTAS I II III

KILLERS ON ELM STREET I II III

JACK BOYZ N DA BRONX I II III

A DOPEBOY'S DREAM I II III

By **Romell Tukes**

LOYALTY AIN'T PROMISED I II

By Keith Williams

QUIET MONEY I II III

THUG LIFE I II III

EXTENDED CLIP I II

By **Trai'Quan**

THE STREETS MADE ME I II III

By **Larry D. Wright**

THE ULTIMATE SACRIFICE I, II, III, IV, V, VI

KHADIFI

IF YOU CROSS ME ONCE

ANGEL I II

IN THE BLINK OF AN EYE

By **Anthony Fields**

THE LIFE OF A HOOD STAR

By Ca$h & Rashia Wilson

THE STREETS WILL NEVER CLOSE

By K'ajji

CREAM I II

By Yolanda Moore

NIGHTMARES OF A HUSTLA I II III

By King Dream

CONCRETE KILLA I II

VICIOUS LOYALTY

By Kingpen

HARD AND RUTHLESS I II

MOB TOWN 251

THE BILLIONAIRE BENTLEYS

By Von Diesel

GHOST MOB

Stilloan Robinson

MOB TIES I II III IV

By SayNoMore

BODYMORE MURDERLAND I II III

By Delmont Player

FOR THE LOVE OF A BOSS

By C. D. Blue

MOBBED UP I II III IV

THE BRICK MAN I II

By King Rio

KILLA KOUNTY

By Khufu

MONEY GAME I II

By Smoove Dolla

A GANGSTA'S KARMA I II

By FLAME

KING OF THE TRENCHES II

by **GHOST & TRANAY ADAMS**

QUEEN OF THE ZOO

By **Black Migo**

GRIMEY WAYS

By Ray Vinci

XMAS WITH AN ATL SHOOTER

Sugar E. Walls

By Ca$h & Destiny Skai

BOOKS BY LDP'S CEO, CA$H

TRUST IN NO MAN

TRUST IN NO MAN 2

TRUST IN NO MAN 3

BONDED BY BLOOD

SHORTY GOT A THUG

THUGS CRY

THUGS CRY 2

THUGS CRY 3

TRUST NO BITCH

TRUST NO BITCH 2

TRUST NO BITCH 3

TIL MY CASKET DROPS

RESTRAINING ORDER

RESTRAINING ORDER 2

IN LOVE WITH A CONVICT

LIFE OF A HOOD STAR

XMAS WITH AN ATL SHOOTER

Sugar E. Walls